THE P
CAPTAIN

by John Davis

Introductory chapters and glossary
by Colin Elliott

Cover design and sketches by Peter Stuckey

Tops'l Books

View from the Cathedral Close at Salisbury where the author of "The Post Captain" went to school.

Contents

Introduction

"The Post Captain" has been described as "the parent of all our nautical novels". It first made its appearance while England was still agog with the news of Trafalgar and Nelson not yet buried.

In the prevailing atmosphere of patriotic naval euphoria this rollicking yarn became a best seller and stayed regularly in demand for the next 40 years.

It is now over 55 years since it was last in print so it is unknown to many modern devotees of sea literature. It is worth revival both for that reason and because, 178 years after its first appearance, "The Post Captain" remains unique and historically valuable.

We are rich in the literature of the sailing navy, both fact and fiction. No other period of English history holds such a grip on the imagination of those with a love of sea and ships.

Captain Frederick Marryat was the first well known naval novelist. Writing with his own successful sea career behind him while wooden walls still kept the Pax Brittanica, he satisfied the Victorian appetite for salty heroes with a high moral tone and had many imitators. In our own century C. S. Forester revived the genre by creating Hornblower, who has since acquired almost as big a 'Band of Brothers' in print as Nelson had at sea, notable among them Dudley Pope's Ramage and Alexander Kent's Bolitho.

The best of these modern novels are marked by a wealth of research into period detail. Sails are trimmed with all the bewildering nomenclature of running rigging, cannon roar to the correct technicalities of 19th century destruction and bare backs are flayed at frequent intervals with the contents of the boatswain's green baize bag—all good fireside adventure and all highly dramatic.

"The Post Captain" is different and unique among sailing navy novels in being funny. It is almost certainly the only surviving contemporary humerous sea story of the Nelson period.

Today it still makes enjoyable reading as a good natured, saucy romp in which encounters with the enemy, punctuated with a little passion on the poop deck, lead to prize money, romance, thwarted rival suitors, a chase to Gretna Green and final wealth and happiness all round. At the same time, being written from first hand observation, it provides a wealth of authentic detail about the period.

The original second sub-title "A View of Naval Society and Manners" is well justified, though the author probably had tongue in cheek when the penned the first sub-title, "The Wooden Walls Well Manned".

Twenty years after its first publication "The Post Captain" was already being referred to by an expert writer on naval affairs, Captain William Glascock, as "an authority to decide the legitimacy of a disputed nautical phrase". Now that the sailing fighting ship, its way of life and its vocabulary have passed far beyond any living memory it is even more valuable on that account.

As for the author of the work, he died forgotten and penniless. Though the book went through ten editions in his lifetime it is doubtful if he received much for them. He may even have been played a dirty trick by his publisher over the first appearance.

So before leaving the reader to enjoy this only surviving comedy of Nelson's navy, let us attempt to rescue John Davis from obscurity. He deserves it.

The Honourable East India Company's ship *Essex* in which John Davis made his first voyage at the age of 11. On her previous voyage the *Essex* had been dismasted by a cyclone in the Indian Ocean and this drawing shows her at anchor in Bombay Harbour after being refitted.

(Copyright National Maritime Museum, Greenwich)

John Davis, the Sailor Afloat

JOHN DAVIS was born at Salisbury, in the shadow of England's tallest cathedral spire, in December 1774. Of his family background he left no information beyond a few odd facts mentioned in passing in some of his writings, but he does say that he was "reared in the lap of opulence" in a house that boasted a large library. It seems fairly certain that he was the John Davis, son of James and Ann Davis, baptised in the parish of St. Edmund in March 1775. James Davis was a woollen draper and a freeholder of land at Lower Woodford.

John went to Dr. Skinner's school in The Close at Salisbury and was then sent to study mathematics at an academy in Burlington Street, London, run by a Mr. Roy, but his main occupation was to devour books of travel and by the age of eleven "nothing would now satisfy me but going to sea and a ship was the idol of my mind". So in 1787 he shipped as a boy on the East Indiaman *Essex*, commanded by Captain Strover, for a voyage to St. Helena, Batavia and China.

For boys of his age to go to sea was common enough at the time and the 18 month voyage did not dull his appetite for more. Inside six months he was off again, this time in the Indiaman *Worcester*, commanded by a very corpulent and timid Captain Hall, bound for Bombay. The surgeon's mate of the *Worcester* was Mungo Park, later to become the famous explorer. Her third mate Mr. Gower had studied astronomy under the great Maskelyne and taught the youngsters in the night watches.

On the voyage young Davis saw action for the first time and this he described in characteristic style some years later in a short "Memoir" which, rather inconsequentially, forms the introduction to a novel on a quite different subject. Nineteenth century publishers were apt to do that sort of thing.

> "In the *Essex*, the chief mate was Ebenezer Roebuck, a man conspicuous for his courage, consummate seamanship and rigid discipline. The chief officer of the *Worcester* was Owen Ellis, a disciple of Roebuck, full of fire, fancy and mischief. Our captain and he did not agree. Hall was timorous; Ellis rash. Hall was uncommonly corpulent; remarkable for the circumference of his belly; and Ellis swore the ship could never

> be in trim, as, by being in the cabin, he brought her down by the stern.
>
> Off the high land of Chaul the *Worcester* was attacked by Angria's pirates. Our captain was scared almost to death.
>
> Ellis saved the ship. He jumped down on the gun deck, and cast loose a midship gun. 'A match here!' said he, while he was pointing the gun with a handspike. The match was brought by the ship's cook from the galley-fire; a man named John Thornton had primed the gun, the chief mate gave it to the Moors in style, and dispersed their musquito fleet. A loud laugh now succeeded the hallooing, bawling, cursing and swearing, that before shook the good ship *Worcester* from stem to stern. For no sooner did the Moor taste our pills than he put his helm up, wore right round upon his heel, and went away before the wind; this was the ship; the ketch, brig and gallivats did the same".

On this voyage the *Worcester* was transporting a hundred East India Company recruits. Among them was a German named Oberstein described by Davis as "of dissipated fortune, but elegant education". On the long voyage Oberstein began to teach Davis French and to fuel his love of literature in general. His memoir paints an almost idyllic picture of ship's boy's life, rather removed from the more common hard tack and bucko mate tales.

> "---in my watch upon deck my station was in the main-top, to haul down the top-gallant studding sail at the approach of a squall, or to go up and hand the royal. For our top-gallant-masts were fidded, and our royal yards rigged across. When the boatswain's mate piped starbowlines, I walked up the main rigging into the top. I always put Le Sage in my pocket; and in the main-top of an East Indiaman, under a cloudless tropical sky, when the breeze was so steady that for days we had no occasion to start either tack or sheet, I began to cultivate the language of the court of Lewis the Fourteenth".

At Bombay, Davis lodged ashore for several months with the family of a tavern keeper named Londwick who spoke only French but had an ample supply of books, so both his French and his knowledge of literature improved. While there his ship made two trading voyages to all the ports on the Malabar Coast and he says he was "engaged in the reduction of Cannalore under General Abercrombie" though how closely his ship was involved in the action we don't know.

On the homeward voyage, during which he landed at the Cape of Good Hope, he crossed tracks, unknowingly, with his brother who was bound for Madras as an East India Company army cadet.

From the St. Edmond registers it seems probable that his brother was named James and a couple of years his senior. He doesn't tell us much, but a sad note tinges the reference in the memoir. His brother, who was promoted lieutenant at the capture of Pondicherry, died at Madras after attaining his captaincy. How large must have seemed the oceans of separation before the 20th century.

Despite his love of the sea Davis, now around 15, was evidently not fired with an ambition to command. Had he been so he would certainly have pursued promotion with the John Company, as the Honourable East India Company was colloquially dubbed, for this was the elite sea service, offering better career prospects than a life in the King's ships, unless what you wanted was the glory and the gamble of prize money.

There is a clue to his reasons in the memoir when he says that his love of belles-letters had always made him "loath the mathematics and other crabbed sciences", which may mean that he had difficulty learning navigation or that literary ambition was more consuming.

Instead young Davis returned to the family home at Salisbury and burrowed in the library where he taught himself Latin and Greek. He stayed there until the beginning of 1793 when he was 17 and the long war with France broke out. Then, in his own words, he was "sent into the Navy". The word "sent" is rather significant for one who once had been so eager to go to sea and doesn't imply much willingness. Failing family fortunes, perhaps following the death of his father, may have been responsible for him needing to seek a living in one of the few ways then open to the sons of gentlemen. About this time it is the name of Mrs. Ann Davis which appears as head of the wool business in surviving Salisbury directories. At any rate John found himself a midshipman in the frigate *Active* under Captain Edmund Nagle.

While the ship was moored in Long Reach the Captain was visited for the day by his famous cousin Edmund Burke who brought his son. John Davis was introduced. Later the *Active* cruised to the Orkneys, the River Elbe and Cadiz where there was another distinguished visitor. Young Lord Holland, nephew of Charles

James Fox, who brought him up, was doing a Grand Tour. The young nobleman had already met Nelson at Leghorn. When he came aboard the *Active* Captain Nagle appointed Midshipman Davis to conduct his lordship on an inspection of the divisions of seamen assembled at the main deck guns. Afterwards there was a party in the cabin which lasted all afternoon, most of which Holland and Davis spent chatting together, for only a couple of years in age separated the Old Etonian peer and the midshipman and both were born in Wiltshire.

The following year, 1794, the entire ship's company of the *Active* shifted into the *Artois*, 44 guns, a brand new frigate which proved to be a crack sailer.

The *Artois* joined a "flying squadron" of six frigates under Sir John Borlase Warren, flying his broad pennant as Commodore in the *Pomone*, 44 guns. The other ships included the *Arethusa*, Captain Sir Edmund Pellew (later Lord Exmouth) and the *Diamond*, Captain Sir Sidney Smith (an archetypal naval hero whose real life exploits would provide material for several Hornblower type stories).

The job of this squadron was to cruise the French coast harrassing enemy shipping, picking off any privateers which might be a danger to English merchantmen and taking whatever prizes it could—a plum assignment in fact because the chances of prize money on this kind of operation were higher than on main fleet duties. This proved to be the case on October 21st 1794 when the squadron gave chase to a French frigate, the *Revolutionnaire* which had been spotted at daybreak.

The *Artois* lived up to her reputation. Davis recorded that "no ship could touch her, whether going large, or close hauled". On this occasion the other five ships were hull down astern within two hours. Soon afterwards the *Artois* overhauled the *Revolutionnaire* and cut her off from the land off Ushant. To do this the *Artois's* crew had to withstand for nearly an hour the sustained fire of the *Revolutionnaire's* stern guns which they did, Davis recalled in later life, "with a kind of sulking indifference" until they could bring their broadside to bear.

Davis' only detailed account of the affair was published, again quite irrelevantly, in the back of a book of poems written 40 years later and dedicated to Lord Holland.

> "My station was at the aftermost gun but two on the quarterdeck, not far from the wheel where Captain Nagle and Lieutenant Oliver stood working the ship and giving

> their orders with perfect calmness and self possession; and though an 18 pounder shot tore up the bulwark which supported the hammock cloths and mortally wounded Lieutenant Craigie of the Marines, yet they betrayed no preposterous sympathy at his fall; a couple of seamen were merely named to carry him below to the cockpit and an action of an hour was conducted without the least confusion or disorder".

The *Artois* had been hotly engaged for 40 minutes before the next ship came up. This was the *Diamond* which was positioned across the stern of the *Revolutionnaire,* but as the naval historian Laird Clowes records "Sidney Smith did not spoil *Artois'* game by firing". Warfare was, after all, still a game for gentlemen.

Shortly after that Capitaine H. A. Thevenard struck his colours. He had put up a creditable resistance and obviously stood no chance against a superior number of ships. He had eight dead and five wounded. The *Artois* had three dead and five wounded.

Sir Sidney Smith hailed Captain Nagle to congratulate him and called: "We envied you blazing away and having it all to yourself". At that moment, Davis recalls, the signal was hoisted for a strange sail in sight and the rest of the squadron gave chase, leaving the *Artois* to her prize which proved to be a fine new ship and was taken into British Navy service.

Captain Nagle was knighted for his bravery. After spending the 10 years before the war on half pay he must have thought this marked the beginning of better things and it did.

Lieutenant Robert Dudley Oliver was rewarded by being appointed commander of the prize. He was made Post Captain eighteen months later and died a full admiral in 1841.

Midshipman Davis must have acquitted himself well too. He was appointed Acting Lieutenant of the *Revolutionnaire* to assist Oliver sail her to Spithead. Prize crew places were usually regarded as a privilege reserved for those who had behaved with credit in the action.

Unfortunately this mark of approval held no promise of future advancement for Davis. Sir Edmund Nagle sympathised with him over the fact that the promotion would not be confirmed, due to the fact that his time in the merchant service could not count towards the six years sea time required of Lieutenants in the Navy. The Lords of the Admiralty had for many years connived at all sorts of fiddles to overcome barriers such as this in their regulations and it must have been a disappointment to Davis that there was no way round in his case.

The following year *Pomone's* squadron was given a new role, providing the naval cover for the abortive attempt to reverse the French Revolution by landing 2,500 French emigré troops on the Quiberon Peninsula where, within a month, they were betrayed, defeated and over half of them slaughtered.

After the withdrawal of the survivors and their 50 transports some of the squadron, including the *Artois,* remained watching French movements on the Brittany coast. On July 31st 1797 while chasing a French frigate off La Rochelle the *Artois* struck a sandbank and was a total wreck.

His commission thus at an end Captain Sir Edmund Nagle went home, married a rich widow and subsequently never again pressed very hard for seagoing appointments. John Davis went back to his books and except as a passenger, never went to sea again.

John Davis, the Author Ashore

For one of so bookish a disposition as Davis life in a man o'war's midshipman's berth, crowded and crude in every sense of the word, must often have been singularly uncongenial, so perhaps he did not altogether regret the abrupt ending of his naval career.

His appetite for travel was not sated however and in January 1798, at 23 years old, he shipped out of Bristol in the *Two Brothers,* a 200 ton snow, for New York.

Before leaving Salisbury he obtained a letter of introduction from Henry Wansey, a noted Wiltshire antiquary and collected a library of 300 books to while away the voyage—which was just as well because the *Two Brothers* was a slow old tub which did not reach New York until March 18th.

For the sake of economy he travelled steerage, which cost him only seven guineas for the passage, plus £3 for provisions. He had travelling companions, "two young gentlemen of my acquaintance". The only other steerage passengers were a Somerset farmer and his housekeeper going to settle in Pennsylvania while the cabin class was occupied by a Unitarian preacher and two merchants. While all the other passengers were miserable, Davis the old salt was able to make himself comfortable by slinging the cot he had brought with him and retiring with his books.

In New York he had a stroke of luck in meeting a bookseller who offered him 200 dollars to translate Bonaparte's Italian Campaigns from the French. That was the beginning of a literary career which blossomed prodigiously in the next half dozen years and he must have written at a tremendous rate because he was also continually on the move. He perhaps burned himself out because the momentum was never regained.

The next four years were spent travelling, mainly on foot, through South Carolina, Georgia, Maryland and Virginia. The journey gave him material for several books to be published later, but en route he produced a couple of novels ("The Farmer of New Jersey" and "The Wanderings of William") several poems and more translations, as well as taking jobs at intervals as a private tutor.

For some of these journeys he had a travelling companion, Dr. de Bow, a medical practitioner who, like Holmes' Dr. Watson, seems to have been able to leave his practise with little notice and disappear into the blue. Twice Davis visited Washington, once to hear President Thomas Jefferson speak in the Capitol and once to apply for a government post on the introduction of Vice President Burr who had become a friend. A misunderstanding prevented the appointment or we might have heard no more of John Davis, the author. As it was he returned to England in 1802, sailing in the American brig *Olive* from Baltimore to Cowes. He recalls in his memoir:

> "I landed from the ship within twelve miles of my mother's home. It commanded a view of the English Channel and the tall English fleet. I did not stay long in Hampshire. I proceeded to London, where my time was divided between pleasure and literature".

Why his mother had moved south we do not know but it is clear that John Davis had not inherited anything of substance and had no other income than that he could earn. This view is re-inforced by the sub-title given to his book of American travels—"In Search of Independence and Settlement"—which was dropped after the first edition.

Judging by the work produced in the next couple of years the division of time in London between pleasure and literature must have been heavily balanced in favour of the latter. He wrote up his American journeys in a book entitled "Travels of Four and a Half Years in The United States" which brought favourable comment from Macaulay and Wordsworth and was attracting new editions in America as late as 1910. This book came out in 1803 under the imprint of a Bristol publisher, a city where Davis must have spent a lot of time after coming home because he was also researching and writing a biography of Thomas Chatterton, a self-educated Bristolian who created a literary sensation in the mid 18th century by "discovering" some lost manuscripts of mediaeval poems—he had of course composed them himself.

In the same period Davis divested himself of another novel with an American background called "Walter Kennedy" and, more importantly in the present context, wrote "The Post Captain". He probably travelled in South Wales before this, since the Welsh scenes in "The Post Captain" have been attested as accurate in local detail. He also went to Berkeley in Gloucestershire to call on Dr. Jenner, the inventor of vaccine innoculation. The good doctor was out, but wrote a letter reproduced in a later book.

Davis was now anxious to be off again and he left the massive "Life of Thomas Chatterton" and "The Post Captain" at No. 111, Cheapside, London with a publisher called Thomas Tegg, to be printed after his departure.

Davis went to Liverpool at the end of 1804 and embarked in the *Cotton Planter* for New York, travelling steerage again. It was not such a comfortable trip as the previous one. His memoir records:

> "I never witnessed severer gales. It was necessary to keep the broad axe sharp, when the ship was lying to, in case she should go on her beam ends; that we might cut away her weather rigging or the masts, in order to enable her to get upon her legs again".

Back in London Thomas Tegg was in no hurry to publish. The "Life of Chatterton" did not in fact appear in the bookshops until 1806. But on the foggy morning of November 6th, 1805 the papers came out with the news of the greatest naval victory of all time and London, by contemporary accounts, both mourned and celebrated.

It may be that Thomas Tegg was just lucky in his timing and that "The Post Captain" was already being printed. On the other hand he surely was not the first, and certainly not the last London publisher to rush through a book whose theme had suddenly become topical. Other factors lend weight to the theory that this is what he did.

"The Post Captain" was in the bookshops by December 1805, price seven shillings. Nelson still lay in state at Greenwich awaiting his January funeral at St. Paul's and the reading public was, hopefully, hungry for some light hearted narrative about the country's glorious Navy.

But wily Thomas Tegg thought they had never heard of an author called John Davis, so he advertised "The Post Captain" as being by somebody they had heard of, Dr. John Moore, an Edinburgh medic, bosom pal of the Duke of Hamilton and then a very fashionable writer. His only claim to a place in history now is as the father of Sir John Moore, the hero of Corunna, whose death gave rise to the famous lines:

> "Not a drum was heard, not a funeral note
> As the corpse to the ramparts we carried"

At the time of Trafalgar all society had heard of Dr. Moore as the author of "Zeluco", "Ellen" and other popular works, but he had been dead three years when his name was borrowed for "The Post Captain". It was a blatant deception because Tegg had never been publisher of any of Moore's works, and the trickery seems to have been carried even further. A reviewer in the "Naval Chronicle" complained that Dr. Moore's name had been *pasted* on to the back of his copy and accused Tegg of "hanging out false colours to get off his crudities".

The deception naturally soured his opinion of the book which he grudgingly praises with one hand and criticises with the other, yet considering it worthwhile enough to give readers a six page extract. "Every page abounds in sea terms, sometimes delivered like a seaman; but there is a vast deal, which betrays the slang of a land-lubber, such as we meet with in masquerades, from cocknies dressed in sailors' jackets and trowsers . . .".

Rumbled or not Tegg continued the deception unabashed and the public apparently lapped it up. There was a second edition in 1806 and a third in 1808. Not until the fifth edition in 1811 did the misleading title page disappear. The real author all this time was in America and there is nothing to show whether he was aware of what Tegg was up to or not, beyond the fact that in 1805 he mentions having written "The Post Captain" during his visit to England. If he was party to the duplicity he would hardly have claimed authorship publicly, but if he was tricked by Tegg he never complained in print.

Thereafter there were further reprintings, properly credited to Davis, at regular intervals down to a tenth edition in 1846 when the pioneering nature of the work was being commented on and its authority as a source of naval phraseology acknowledged.

Just to round off the story of this bit of jiggery-pokery some people confused Dr. J. Moore with a J. J. Moore, a naval officer who had written a "British Mariner's Vocabulary" in 1801, so that at one time "The Post Captain" had the distinction of being listed in the British Museum catalogue as by three different authors at the same time.

While Tegg was up to his tricks, Davis was beavering away in America translating a French travel book and writing an historical novel published in late 1805 entitled "The First Settlers in Virginia", which he dedicated to Dr. Jenner. Though this was advertised as an historical novel it was in fact an only slightly fictionalised account of the romantic but true story of the Indian Princess Pocahontas who begged her people to spare the life of Captain Smith, leader of the early 17th century colonists at James Town and who subsequently married another officer with whom she returned to live in England where she sadly died at Gravesend in Kent, where there is still a memorial to her.

It was in this volume that Davis included the memoir previously quoted. For a young man of 30 beginning to build some reputation as a writer it has a strangely wearisome note:

> "I however have no further desire to travel. It is true I should much like to cross the Atlantic again, but then that would be to go home. When the cold turf presses against my breast, I hope it will be one dug out of the vallies of my native land".

These sound like the words of somebody who is either ill or overworked or disillusioned and homesick, but he stayed in the United States for the best part of the next 20 years. Unfortunately his life seems a blank in this period.

He turns up again in 1823, back in Salisbury, where the firm of Brodie and Dowday published his epic narrative poem "The American Mariners", described as "a vindication of the American character from the aspersions of the quarterly reviewers, to which is added the Naval Annals, an impartial account of the actions fought during the late war".

The war in question was that of 1812 when the Royal Navy did rather less well against the young United States Navy than might have been expected of the victors of Trafalgar.

The poem ran to 4,442 lines, apart from the equally lengthy "Annals" recounting in prose the individual naval engagements of the conflict. It was dedicated to Robert Southey who at some time had commented favourably on Davis's work. Though the poem makes deterring reading today it is rich with the author's footnotes explaining contemporary naval terms and practise and would repay study. Its composition must have accounted for quite a lot of the blank period in the author's life.

Poetry was by now the erstwhile sailor's main preoccupation. He moved to Winchester where he set up as a bookseller in King's Gate Street and there in 1836 published himself a volume of his own verse compositions. These were all historical narrative poems connected with Winchester, relating, for instance, the stories of St. Cross Hospital and the Hall of the Hundred Men and incidents in the life of the cathedral and castle.

But neither poetry nor bookselling brought in enough to live on, even for a bachelor frugal enough to make a habit of travelling steerage. This is evident from an advertisement tucked away at the back of the slim pocket volume of poems announcing that J. Davis, Bookseller "proposes to instruct a few young gentlemen in the more useful branches of the mathematics, comprehending the pure elements of geometry, plain and spherical trigonometry and leading properties of Conic Sections and the principles of the differential and integral Calculus. The mathematical use of both Globes and (if required) the Greek and Latin Classics, together with English and French literature".

Something must have altered his earlier hatred of "the mathematics and other crabbed sciences". In fact in the same book of poems in another brief out of context note he recounts what "lively pleasure" he had when he "embraced the mathematics under Mr. Roy" at the Burlington Street Academy 50 years before. Unfortunately this retrospective enthusiasm for "the mathematics" was of no avail. In the British Library copy of the poems ("St. Cross, etc. with the execution of the Earl of Kent before the Castle Gates at Winchester") there is a sad pencilled note beneath the advertisement. It states: "Only one pupil ever obtained—now in the London University".

By now poor Davis was becoming bankrupt, despite the fact that several of his books were still being re-published, including "The Post Captain", now in its tenth edition. At the age of 68 he was nominated by Queen Victoria to a place in the Charterhouse, the London almshouse founded in 1611 to provide, as it still does, for 80 old men of gentle birth who had "fallen on evil days" and he was sworn in there as a "poor brother" by the Bishop of London on December 5th 1843.

A report of the event in the Athenaeum magazine that month said that he was "entirely destitute and without any other means than those supplied by private benevolence". The writer quoted Macaulay's praise of Davis's work and recalled the popularity of "The Post Captain" which he described as "the parent of all our nautical novels".

Even in the poor house Davis did not let his pen stay idle. He let his mind wander back to the happy days of adolescent adventure and wrote a novel about a young boy's first voyage in a John Company ship. It appeared in 1847 under the title "Jack Ariel, or Life Aboard an Indiaman" and it was dedicated to Macaulay the poet and historian who could well have been the person who influenced his nomination to the Charterhouse. He had the satisfaction of seeing "Jack Ariel" go into a second edition before he died on April 24th 1854, aged 79, after 11 years in the Charterhouse. Hopefully the proceeds afforded the author a few comforts in his last years. He was buried in a plot reserved for the Poor Brothers at Tower Hamlets Cemetery at an expense of £5. 15s. 0d. which the Registrar of Charterhouse paid.

King's Gate, Winchester, close to which Davis had his bookseller's business and tried unsuccessfully to run a school for young gentlemen.
(Copyright Colin Elliott)

Made Post! The Coveted Prize

No happier title could have been found for a successful naval novel than the one John Davis chose, "The Post Captain". Few other subjects occupied the minds of the 4,500 officers on the Navy List during the Revolutionary Wars quite so much as the acquisition of that significant rank.

No-one spoke then of being promoted to Captain. It was always "I am made Post", or "Henry has been made Post" and usually accompanied with the same jubilation that Lieutenant Echo displays in Davis's story: "Oh! Seas and skies! I am so happy. I am made Post". Because right down to the middle of the 19th century the acquisition of post rank meant much more than the attainment of four gold rings does in the modern navy.

A modern officer promoted Captain, R.N. can be justly proud of having reached a high rung of the ladder, but on the way he will have negotiated a number of rungs for which he must have gained experience, passed examinations and convinced superiors of his merit. After that he might go on or he might stay put, according to his ability and opportunities. But a man "made post" in the sailing navy could not be stopped. By the rules of the game he had only to stay alive to end up Admiral of the Fleet.

This strange state of affairs led to all kinds of ploys and subterfuges which permeated Georgian society and influenced the lives of boys destined for the navy when they were hardly out of the nursery. To understand why it was quite so important we must examine the way in which the navy then recruited and advanced its officers.

Right down to the end of the Napoleonic Wars more than 80 per cent of all officers first joined the King's Navy (they didn't say Royal Navy much in those days), as they had for over a century, as captain's servants.

Every commanding officer at that time was allowed personal servants, paid and victualled by the Navy, on a scale of four for every hundred men in the crew, which meant that most captains of ships of the line had about 16 servants. If the captain happened also to be a knight, baronet or peer the number was doubled! As no man, however self indulgent, could possibly want quite so many personal attendants there had grown up a practice over the previous hundred years and more of filling the spare places with their own sons, the sons of friends and relations, and the sons of the friends and relations of aynone they wished to oblige and who might be relied upon to scratch their back in return at some future date.

Occasionally since the time of Pepys the Admiralty had taken half hearted steps to regulate this system, which virtually took personnel selection out of its hands, but vested interests were strong and Their Lordships left well alone. They did make one ruling however. They said that all the entrants must be at least 13 years of age except the sons of naval officers who could join at 11.

Almost everybody disobeyed this order and Their Lordships spent over a hundred years pretending not to notice. Boys as young as eight were signed on as captain's servants. They mostly didn't go to sea, but stayed with Mama or at school, but their names went on the Muster Book of the ship whose captain had agreed to have them as "servant" so that they could truthfully say in later years that they were "borne on the books of HMS So-and-So from 1785" or whatever it was. This little fiddle was invaluable in the race towards that coveted, critical step of Post Captain because the period they were "borne on the books", whether actually aboard or not, counted as "sea-time".

By the time he was 15 the captain's servant could become a midshipman. Again he relied on the patronage of an obliging commanding officer to take him, but no particular fiddles were necessary at this stage. When he wanted the next step to Lieutenant it was a different matter and the ambitious "middie" had every reason to want this step as soon as possible. Becoming Lieutenant was the only promotion in an officer's career governed by Admiralty examination and in order to be examined a candidate must have clocked up six years' sea time and have reached the age of 20. So the youngster who had the good fortune to have been "borne on the books" from an early age was well away with the first condition. As for the age stipulation, nobody took much notice of that. There were porters at the Admiralty building who did a brisk trade in bogus birth certificates. One examining admiral on inspecting a certificate was heard to mutter how odd it was that the ink had not dried in 20 years! Others squared their consciences by writing in their notes that "the candidate *appears* to be 20 years of age". So with the help of that servant sea time, real or fictitious, and a fib about his age a young chap could become a Lieutenant well before 20.

Sometimes the lieutenant's examination was dispensed with when an acting promotion had been made at sea after an action and we have seen how the author of "The Post Captain" was disappointed because his acting rank could not be confirmed as he had not been "borne on the books" of a King's ship, even though he was a seasoned seaman in the merchant service.

Once an officer had got his Lieutenant's Passing Certificate there was nothing then standing between him and the important rise to Post Captain. There was no examination or interview. There was no minimum period of service stipulated. Technically he could be made post the day after passing for lieutenant. There was no intermediate rank. Commanders were not invented until the late 18th century and for a long time the title was used to cover an "appointment" to command a small vessel such as an armed cutter rather than a "rank" and the intermediate step was not obligatory, though it became more common in later years. The one qualification that was supremely required was "interest", or as we should say now "influence" or "pull".

In the absence of the right family connections this meant cultivating the acquaintance of some politician, or perhaps a nobleman with a rotten borough or two at his disposal, who would become your "patron" and approach, sometimes even pester, the First Lord of the Admiralty for you. The right party loyalties counted for a lot and many hopes were dashed by each change of government.

Nelson was made Post Captain at the age of 20, having been promoted Lieutenant at 18½. He had already demonstrated his ability, but also had an uncle in the right place and around 20 was quite a usual age for those who had access to the right ear to be "posted". The record was probably held by John Rodney, the son of Admiral Lord Rodney whose father saw to it that he was promoted Post Captain just five weeks after being made Lieutenant and when he was still 16!

Incredibly this crazy system produced the men responsible for the flowering of the British Navy in the 18th and 19th centuries, and in fact most of the great names of British naval history, possibly because there was such a huge pool of officers available. Even at the height of the Napoleonic wars jobs could only be found for two thirds of the men on the Navy List while the rest fretted at home on half pay, a sharp contrast to the situation on the lower deck where the Navy was so desparate to swell the ranks of its 100,000 seamen that the press gangs were constantly employed to take men forcibly.

Little wonder then that Georgian society had such a keen interest in the scramble to be "made Post", especially when we consider the benefits that followed. They included an increase in pay from £7 to £28 a month and the chance of commanding a frigate or a ship-of-the-line with a much increased share of any prize money, but above all the certain knowledge that one day, barring accidents, you could be addressed as Admiral. Because for all ranks beyond Post Captain the Admiralty had long had a rule that advancement should be by seniority only and no damned nonsense about merit. For once this was an instruction everybody obeyed.

When an admiral died the Post Captain at the top of the list chronologically automatically moved up into the flag list. Hence the desire to be on the captains list as early as possible. No wonder the popular officers' toast was "Here's to a bloody war and a sickly season". Even Nelson, had he survived, would not have become Admiral of the Fleet, the most senior flag rank, until he was 86 years old, 39 years after Trafalgar, which he fought as Vice-Admiral of the White.

At the time of this story the Navy had an even larger proportion of unemployed admirals than lesser officers. Less than 20 per cent of them had jobs. In fact the great majority of them never hoisted their flags at sea at all. Still they were luckier than the large number of men who had made it to Post Captain, but not early enough in life. That great authority on the social history of the Navy, the late Professor Michael Lewis, described them graphically as "these gallant old men, clinging to life in the hope that the Flag would come before the Funeral".

It took the Admiralty many more years to rid itself of the system and to come round to the idea of retiring its officers on pensions instead of keeping them all on half pay and being automatically promoted by seniority and theoretically available for service. When that happened the term Post Captain itself became redundant and we ended up with the modern Captain R.N., but even then the expressions "Post Captain" and "made Post" could still be heard being used occasionally in the Royal Navy right up to the 2nd World War.

The word captain needs no explanation but why the word post attaches to it may. This originated from much further back in naval history when there was officially no such concept as a regular professional naval officer, just as in centuries previously there had been no regular navy ships, only private vessels requisitioned in time of war. Commissions held good only for one appointment and so a man was sent to a "post" as "captain" of a particular ship. When he came ashore again he reverted to plain "Mr.", but human vanity being what it is the practise emerged of hanging on to the title, until by the time of this novel it was universal usage, though still technically incorrect until 1860 when commissions were re-worded to cover regular continuing service.

When Davis wanted a model for the central character of "The Post Captain" he did not have to stir his imagination very deep. His boisterous Captain Brilliant owes much to the only Post Captain Davis was able to observe at close quarters, Captain Nagle of the *Active* and the *Artois.*

Nagle had stuck to the letter of the law. He didn't enter the Navy till he was 13 and was a full 20 when he passed for lieutenant in 1777. Despite his political relationships he wasn't made post for another five years. At the outbreak of war he had been on half pay for 10 years and was 36 when he commissioned the *Active.*

It would not have been dull serving under him. We have seen that there were parties in the cabin when there were visitors like Burke and Lord Holland. Furthermore Nagle was an Irishman of easy going nature noted, according to the Dictionary of National Biography, for his "rollicking good humour" and his "great good nature and simplicity of mind". Captain Brilliant is surely only aspects of Captain Nagle in caricature, with the Irish bit reserved to create Captain Tempest.

When he came ashore after the sinking of the *Artois* in 1797 and married his rich widow he does not seem to have pressed his kinsman Edmund Burke to use his "interest" to secure him plum appointments, any more than Captain Brilliant was in any hurry to get back to sea. All his postings after that were for very brief periods to not very active appointments, including the command of the Sea Fencibles, a sort of maritime Home Guard, in Sussex. He set up his headquarters for this in Brighton in 1801 where he met the Prince of Wales.

Nagle was just the sort of boon companion that Prinny enjoyed. They became lifelong friends. By 1805 Nagle's name had reached the top of the Captains' List and in November of that year he gained the first rung of the flag list as Rear Admiral of the Blue, a direct result of Nelson's death when everybody under him moved up one. He did fly his flag for a brief time aboard the *Inconstant* and again as C. in C. at Leith in 1810 after he had become Vice Admiral, and in 1813 he had a year as Governor of Newfoundland. The Governorship was at that period a sinecure probably requiring no more than a token visit to the colony.

In 1814 when Prinny was Prince Regent he appointed Nagle as his aide-de-camp for the grand review of the fleet at Spithead by Allied monarchs and when the Prince ascended the throne as George IV in 1820 Sir Edmund Nagle, now full Admiral by seniority, became Groom of the Bedchamber to his king.

It is tempting to think that they might have had a good laugh together over the preposterous story written by that young whippersnapper of a midshipman that Nagle had aboard during his days as Post Captain.

The frigate *Active,* the first ship in which John Davis served under Captain Nagle, depicted in stays off the Isle of Wight in an engraving made by C. Bowles in 1783 when she returned home after taking part in the Battle of Trincomalee. She was wrecked in 1796 but there were many more *HMS Actives*. The name was popular with the British navy and has been used for at least a couple of dozen ships since the middle of the 18th century. The 18th of the name, a corvette sold off in 1906, had the distinction of being the last man o'war to leave Portsmouth harbour under sail.

The title page from the third edition of "The Post Captain" printed in 1808. The name of the true author does not appear, but the publisher is ambiguous in deceitfully ascribing the novel to someone with a better selling name. He identifies Dr. Moore by his previous works without actually printing the name, but he added the name by hand to some review copies. The reviewer in the Naval Chronicle was not deceived. He wrote:

"We fear that this volume, which is not without its merit, has been made up to impose on the credulity of the naval profession, and more particularly of the public in general; by having Dr. Moore's name pasted on its back. Had it been really the production of the author of Zeluco, we would gladly have eked out a seven shilling piece from our half-pay to purchase it. But Mr. Thomas Tegg, the publisher, ought not in these hard times to hang out false colours, to get off his crudities".

The Post-Captain;

OR,

THE WOODEN WALLS WELL MANNED;

comprehending

A VIEW OF NAVAL SOCIETY and Manners.

BY THE AUTHOR OF 'EDWARD;' 'A VIEW OF SOCIETY IN FRANCE;' &c.

The Third Edition, corrected.

Think you now behold
Upon the hempen tackle ship-boys climbing;
Hear the shrill whistle which doth order give
To sounds confused: behold the threaden sails,
Born by th'invisible and creeping wind,
Draw the huge bottom through the furrow'd sea,
Breasting the lofty surge. Shakespeare.

LONDON:

PUBLISHED BY THOMAS TEGG, 111, CHEAPSIDE:

Printed by Hazard and Carthew, 49, Beech-street.

1808.

Sir Edmund Nagle, the model for Davis' Post Captain, portrayed during the 1820's after his promotion to full Admiral and when he was Groom of the Bedchamber to George the Fourth. The original portrait was by William Corden. This engraving from it by William Ward was published by William Sams, "book and printseller to the royal family", in 1830, the year in which both Nagle and the King died.

The Post Captain

Chapter 1

THE sun had just streaked the eastern hemisphere with his rays, when the commander of a frigate, which was cruising in the British Channel, awoke; and giving a monstrous yawn, called to the sentry at the cabin-door to pass the word for the steward. The sentry was walking to and fro under the half-deck, armed with a huge cutlass, which for more than a year had not slept in a scabbard; and, on hearing the order, he applied his hands to his mouth, vociferating with the lungs of a stentor, "Pass the word there for the captain's steward!"

Our Captain next took a miniature from under his pillow, which he seemed to contemplate with peculiar delight; sighing and soliloquizing as he hung over it enamoured: "Can any face," cried he, "be more angelic? Such top-lights! Or can any form be more ravishing? Such a pair of cat-heads! And, oh! what hair! By——, one might take a sheep-shank in it! Blow my good breeze! Fill all my sails! driver and ring-tail, spritsail and sprit-topsail! Royals and sky-scrapers! flying jib and jib of jibs! Waft me, oh waft me to the arms of Cassandra!"

The captain now bellowed for the Steward.

"Sir!" said the steward.

"How many knots does the ship go?" "Five, sir."

"And how is the wind?"

"A little upon the quarter, sir."

"Are all the reefs out?"

"No, sir, there is one reef in."

"What lieutenant has the watch?"

"Mr Hurricane, sir."

"Desire him to step below."

Mr Hurricane, on hearing the summons, threw off his *grego,* that is, his great-coat, and calling to the quarter-master, told him to take it below. He then went to the compass, and having ascertained the course of the ship, and the direction of the wind, he ordered the helmsman to steer small, dispatched hands aloft to shake out the reefs; and, grasping his speaking-trumpet, descended into the cabin.

"Mr Hurricane," said the captain, "I hope all the reefs are out?"

"The top-men, sir," replied the lieutenant, "are aloft shaking them out."

"Is there any land in sight?" added the captain.

"The master," replied the lieutenant, "says he can see land broad upon the bow; but I, sir, am of opinion it is only cape fly-away."

"Well," said the captain, "make all the sail you can upon the ship, and in a short time we shall be able to determine the fact."

The lieutenant went upon deck. "Mr Echo," said he to a midshipman, "send the after-guard aft here, to hoist the main-topsail."

"Aye, aye! sir," cried Mr Echo, who in concert with half-a-dozen other weekly-account gentlemen, thus vociferated for several minutes at the break of the quarter-deck: "Boatswain's mate! boatswain's mate! I say, you boatswain's mate! send the after-guard aft here to the main-topsail-haliards. Corporal of marines! send the marines aft on the quarter-deck, to clap on the main-topsail-haliards. Master at arms! go down below and send all the idlers up! Send all the idlers up! Do you hear, there, master at arms? Send all the idlers up! Stewards and servants, barbers and sweepers, cook's mates and cook-mate's ministers; doctor's mates and loblolly-boys! After-guard! I don't see the after-guard coming aft! Where's the captain of the after-guard? Pass the word there in the waist for the captain of the after-guard!"

The people now came upon deck, the topsails were hoisted, and the walk of the ship was considerably increased. Seven bells were now struck, the hammocks were piped up, and the quarter-master stood at the nettings to receive them from the sailors.—And now came upon deck the doctor, the purser, and lieutenant of marines, bloated with eating, drinking, and sleeping.

"Good morrow-morning to you, gentlemen," said the lieutenant. "How are you all upon an average?"

"The tiller," said Mr Nipcheese the purser, "made such a thundering noise all night, that I could only procure eleven hours' sleep."

"I pity you," said the lieutenant; "you get no more sleep than a ground-tier-butt."

"And I," said Mr Gallipot, the doctor, "was obliged to get up in the night to go to the round-house."

"Shocking!" cried the lieutenant, "to be taken aback, and not able to box you ship off!"

"And I," said Mr Easy, the lieutenant of marines, "was compelled to rise at midnight and drink a glass of cold water."

"Damnable!" said the lieutenant, "then your coppers were hot!"

"I am getting the better of my sea-sickness," said the purser: "Occupation! occupation! throw but a stone, the giant dies!"

"Yes," rejoined the lieutenant; "and now you will be occupied *in making dead men chew tobacco.*"

"I am an old voyager!" exclaimed the doctor.

"What!" said the lieutenant; "have you got a timber-head in the ship?"

"I have been at sea before," replied the doctor.

"Yes," said the lieutenant; "you have been at Chelsea, at Battersea; and, I dare say, in the Marshalsea."

The conversation was here interrupted by an uproar in the waist, where Mr Echo, the midshipman, was menacing death to the boy of his mess, and belabouring him over the shoulders with the end of the topsail-sheet.

"Murder! murder!" cried the boy; "it was not my fault. The ship took a lee-lurch, and the kettle fetched way."

"What's the matter here, Mr Echo?" cried the lieutenant. "Has the boy forgot to break up the treble refined sugar; or did he omit to beat the dust out of the Turkey carpet?"

"His kettle is capsized, sir," replied Mr Echo; "and we shall be obliged to breakfast upon burgoo, out of the ship's copper. Nor is that all: the hawbuck has not rolled up a single hammock."

"How could I?" said the boy: "the gentlemen did not turn out before the bell rung for eight o'clock."

"You did not rouse them," said the midshipman.

"Yes, sir," answered the boy, "I roused them a dozen times. I affronted Mr Gale. He had turned in all standing with his boots on; and he swore that if I named him again, he would jump down my throat."

"No replies, sir," said Mr Echo, "you are in a king's ship. Jump down for the tureen, and fill it with burgoo. I saw the doctor's mates go just now to the coppers: if you don't bear a hand, there will be none left for the officers."

"Faith, sir," said the boy, "if that is the case, I must bear a fist indeed. Those doctor's mates eat more than any men in the ship. I saw Mr Ipechacuana eat a pound of shark one day before dinner, just by way of taking the sharp edge off his stomach. Here I go like a rigger!"

Chapter 2

CAPTAIN BRILLIANT having dressed himself, went upon the quarter-deck, where the first lieutenant was walking, in company with the doctor, the purser, the marine officer, and a midshipman. The midshipman, on perceiving the captain, immediately went to leeward.

"A fine morning, Mr Hurricane," said the captain.

"Very fine, sir," answered the lieutenant.

"Well, doctor," said the captain, "how do you carry on the war? Have you recovered you stomach?"

"Yes, sir," replied the doctor, "my organs of digestion are restored to their proper tone; and my stomach loaths no longer its diurnal food."

"Does the doctor eat his allowance, Mr Nipcheese?" said the captain.

"Yes, sir," cried the purser, "he picked the plums for the gun-room pudding last banyan-day, and eat more than half of what I had served out."

"When our pudding, sir," exclaimed the lieutenant, "was put upon the table the plums, I will vouch, were not within hail of each other."

"Ha! ha! " laughed the captain; "when the doctor again undertakes to pick the plums, you must make him whistle the whole time."

Mr Echo, the midshipman, now approached the lieutenant, and bowing with much politeness, acquainted him that it was eight o'clock by the glass. "Very well, Mr Echo," replied the lieutenant; "tell the boatswain's mate to pipe to breakfast."

The bell was now rung for eight o'clock; the glass was turned; the quarter-master and the man at the helm were relieved; the boatswain's mate piped to breakfast, and the air was impregnated with the fumes of burgoo.

The gun-room steward now came up the companion-ladder, to summon the officers to their morning repast; and the doctor, the purser, and the officer of marines descended into the lower regions. In half an hour more, Mr Tafferell, the second lieutenant, made his appearance on the quarter-deck; when Mr Hurricane, together with the midshipman of the morning-watch, accompanied the captain into the cabin; where they found coffee *sans* cream, and toast, and potted beef, and tongue sliced *à la* Vauxhall.

It is with a hesitating hand that I dwell so minutely on the breakfast. Such diminutive observations may be said to lessen the dignity of writing; and though necessary towards the completion of the picture, rarely pass without censure.

It is not every reader that is acquainted with the cabin of a frigate; and it will, therefore, require no apology to take a slight survey of the apartment in which the guests had assembled.

On one side, a row of these *mortal engines, whose rude throats could counterfeit the dread clamours of Jove*; or, in plain language, four eighteen-pounders, on both sides, turned their breeches on the company. The after (back) part of the room admitted light through windows of large dimensions, and looked upon the billows curling their monstrous heads; while a bulk-head, or wainscot, forward, divided the cabin from the half-deck.

"The swell," said captain Brilliant, "is, I think, going down."

"Yes, sir," said the lieutenant, "there is not such a bubbling sea as there was."

"The ship has not much motion."

"No, sir; she rolls very little."

"We will exercise the great guns after breakfast."

"It will be a good opportunity, sir."

"We will fire with the locks, Mr Hurricane: I have a favorable opinion of them."

"It shall be done, sir."

"Our carronades are warm pieces, and they throw a shot pretty far."

"They are famous, sir, in close action."

Here some person knocked at the cabin-door, and the steward going to it, returned to the table with a bundle of papers.

"The gentlemen, sir," said he, "have sent you their day's works."

"Very well," replied the captain; "put them in the quarter-gallery."

Mr Hurricane and the midshipman having sufficiently regaled their palates, made a ship-shape bow to captain Brilliant, and left the house of feasting.

The captain now vociferated for the steward *to clear the decks*; and, having taken a few turns up and down the cabin, apparently lost in profound thought; he passed under the half-deck, and ascended the companion-ladder.

The jolly-boat was lowered down from the davits abaft; a cask was carried out to the distance of a mile from the ship; and captain

Brilliant himself had taken a match in his hand to fire the first gun, when the man stationed at the fore-topsail-yard, called out, "A sail right a-head!"

Every thing now took a different turn. The cask lay neglected; the boat was hoisted up; sail was made on the ship, and the main-deck cleared for action.

But the sail in sight was an easy prize. She proved to be an English West-India-man, that had been captured a few hours before by a French seventy-four cut down.

Captain Brilliant immediately clapped Mr Echo, the midshipman, with six hands on board of her, and was about to shape his course after the enemy, when Mr Hurricane, who returned with the boat, informed him, there was an old gentleman with a beautiful young wife on board the prize, who entreated to be taken into the frigate; for the Frenchmen had plundered them of all the fresh provisions, and left nothing but salt junk.

"Is the lady pretty?" said the captain.

"She is the most beautiful creature, sir," replied the lieutenant, "I ever saw with my eyes. The *Venus* frigate has not got so fair a head."

"Then bear a-hand," cried the captain, "and bring her on board. In the mean time we will rig out the studding-sail booms. Up there! topmen!"

The boat shoved off gain, and in a few minutes returned with Mr Factor and his lady. The husband on the verge of sixty; the wife about seventeen.

Captain Brilliant stretched out his hand to the lady, and helped her up the side; when with much sweetness of manner, she thanked him for his politeness, and congratulated herself upon being emancipated from a barbarous enemy.

The sails were now trimmed fore and aft; the foretack was brought to the cat-head, and the weather clue-garnet of the mainsail was hauled up.

"There she walks through it!" exclaimed captain Brilliant, looking over the side. "Glory! glory! Blow, my sweet breeze!"

While the captain's attention was thus occupied, that of Mrs Factor was engrossed by the graceful manliness of his figure. She could not but make a secret comparison between the vigorous, well-proportioned limbs of the captain, and the tottering spider-shanks of her husband. She was all eye; and a sigh which distended her half-denuded bosom, seemed to announce that illicit love had already taken possession of her heart.

In about an hour and a half, a sail was descried from the mast-head; and preparations were made for action with redoubled energy. The bulk-head of the cabin was knocked down; the yards were slung with chains, and the surgeon arranged his instruments and dressings in the cockpit.

"Fore topmast-head there!" cried the captain.

"Sir!" replied the man aloft.

"What does she look like?"

"She looks, sir, like a whacking frigate."

"Can you see her teeth?"

"Yes, sir; she has a very heavy tier of teeth."

"Steady!" cried the captain to the man at the helm.—"Mr Hurricane!"

"Sir!"

"Get the tompions out of the guns, fore and aft."

"Aye! aye! sir!"

It was now time for the young lady to be conducted to a place of safety; an office that the captain undertook to perform; for Mr Factor had complained of a pain in his bowels, and had already sought the company of the doctor in the lowermost recess of the ship.

"Sweet captain!" cried Mrs Factor, as our hero handed her below; "you are going to seek reputation in the mouth of the cannon!"

"It is only, madam, my duty."

"If prayers, captain, can avert the danger that threatens you, no shot shall come near you. For with uplifted hands I will implore Providence to shield you from harm."

"Only smile upon me, and I am proof against all shot!"

"Good heaven! you talk so carelessly, one would think there was no danger to be apprehended from guns."

"There lies more danger in that eye, than in the lower-deck, upper-deck, quarter-deck, and fore-castle guns of the largest seventy-four."

Mrs Factor made no reply: but she sighed, and looked a great deal more. The captain took a tender farewell of her, and returned upon deck.

In another half-hour, the *Desdemona* had come within gun-shot of the strange sail; and the private signal which she hove out not being answered, the colours were hoisted, and the captain told the master to clap him alongside of the enemy.

"A noble frigate!" exclaimed captain Brilliant, as he reconnoitered her through his glass. "She shews her teeth bravely! Stand by, my boys!"

"All ready, sir" cried the men.

But, as the proverb says,There is many a slip between the cup and the lip. The supposed enemy, instead of shewing French, hoisted American colours; and thus were the hopes of British valour disappointed for the time.

"A Jonathan! by the hookey!" exclaimed captain Brilliant.

"Pork and molasses!" cried lieutenant Hurricane. "I though all fighting had been over in the Jerseys."

Captain Brilliant took his speaking-trumpet.

"Hoay! the ship a-hoy!"

"Holloa!"

"What ship is that?"

"The *Rattlesnake*! United States' man-of-war!"

"Have you seen any thing of a French seventy-four cut down?"

"Yes! She is now in chase of a man-of-war brig. She is going large before the wind."

"Thank you! thank you! Square away the yards here! Haul the mainsail up!"

Both frigates cheered, and parted company.

Whether the French ship enjoyed a good pair of heels, or whether the American captain had misrepresented her situation, it is not for the humble historian of this page to determine. But, after a fruitless search of eight hours, no enemy could be found, and only the water and sky were to be seen, when the sun had sunk beneath the horizon.

Chapter 3

MR FACTOR now came upon deck, not supporting but supported by, his black-eyed spouse, who smiled loves and graces as she ascended the companion-ladder.

Mr Factor's bowels were less painful, for the danger was over; but he looked more like a ghost than one of this world.

Captain Brilliant was leaning over the taffarel, enjoying his recollections. Flora ran towards him.

"Oh, captain!" cried Flora; "I am so glad to see you safe! When I was down in the *cellar,* and the surgeon displayed his dressings, I could think of nothing but heads, and legs, and arms, flying about in the air."

"And it is all for your charming sex," whispered the captain, "that sailors thus expose their lives. Assured that courage alone can merit the fair, I would fight the ship on my stumps, and never strike my colours while there was a shot left in the locker."

"I always loved sailors," cried Flora.

"You may know I am a sailor," said the captain, "by the hardness of my hand. But my heart is of a different nature; a glance from a black eye always lights it into a flame."

"Heigho!" sighed Flora; "I know my heart is strangely agitated."

"And mine," said the captain, "moves up and down like a brig's boom in a calm. To make it lie still, I must have recourse to a parbuckle."

"I pray you unhand me," whispered Flora: "Mr Factor is coming this way."

"Flora!" faultered the merchant; "Flora! what are you doing there? Why don't you come and give me your arm? You know that in my weak state, the *rocking* of the ship is almost death to me."

"I am coming, my dear."

"Here help me below. I want you to put me to bed. Have you hung up the curtains, as I told you?"

"My dear, don't go to bed yet, I imagine tea will be ready soon. A cup of tea will restore you."

"I can't drink tea; it does not agree with me."

"Then, I will make you, my dear, a little panado."

"What kind of panado?"

"The same kind, my dear, that Quasheeba made for me at Martha Bre, when you thought I was going [to] lie-in. You tasted it at my bedside, and said it was excellent."

"Well; help me below." "Yes, my dear."

The happy pair descended.

"A precious husband!" exclaimed captain Brilliant. "There is nothing of him left but ribs and trucks. His coat fits him like a purser's shirt upon a handspike."

"He told me, sir," said the lieutenant, "that he had been a great traveller."

"Granted!" cried the captain. "I dare say he has doubled cape horn."

"He tops the officer over his wife, sir."

"A son of a sea-cook! if he was to fall overboard, I would not heave him a rope."

"We shall have yet, sir, perhaps, to sew him up in his hammock."

"The sooner he goes over the standing part of the main sheet the better."

The steward, at this juncture came to acquaint the captain that tea was ready.

"Tea!" exclaimed captain Brilliant. "I wish to make a better land-fall. Stretch along the eating haliards! You are determined we shall not escape being raked fore and aft."

The captain and his lieutenant now walked up and down the quarter-deck.

"Hurricane," said the captain, "I am very glad you brought the young lady on board. I hate to see a priest. A ship never gets safe to port that has a priest in her; but a fine girl is a charming acquisition."

"Should the merchant and his lady, sir, incommode you, I will willingly give up my cabin to them in the gun-room."

"I thank you kindly! Take a severe turn there! I would rather have them in my cabin. If the wife was old and ugly, they should descend into the gunroom; but, as she is young and pretty, I will keep them aloft."

"Is not Flora, sir, a French name?"

"Yes it is; it is Creole French."

"But the lady, sir, is English. Her husband at least said so."

"He may tell that to the marines, but the sailors will not believe him."

"I think, sir, she is a Creole."

"You may tell it by the peak of her mizen."

"How fine she had rigged herself, when I brought her, sir, on board."

"She was under a press of sail. She had royals set; sky-scrapers, moon-rakers, and a cursed god above all."

"Will it not be necessary, sir, to put down the lady as a passenger?"

"Yes."

"She has a delicate skin, sir."

"Faith! she has. She is fair as driven charcoal."

The steward again appeared, to announce that the cold meat was laid out in the cabin.

"Very well," said the captain. "Get some wine to pass. Come, Hurricane, let us board the beef in the smoke."

The day was succeeded by a beautiful night. The full moon arose in solemn majesty, whilst a moderate breeze swelled the bosoms of the sails.

Mr Factor, feeling a nausea from the motion of the ship, ascended the deck with his youthful spouse, to enjoy the fresh air; while captain Brilliant sat over his wine with the first lieutenant, in his cabin.

"Another bottle of wine here!" cried captain Brilliant. "You, steward! don't you see this bottle is a marine. The lights, I suppose, are put out: they are handing up powder out of the magazine. Faith! Hurricane, our lady passenger is a fine girl. She has a good pair of cat-heads!"

"Yes, sir, she is nice and bluff about the bows."

"It was a great sacrifice in so young a girl, to get spliced to so old a man."

"Yet, sir, she says she loves him dearly."

"Avast there! She may tell the marines that; but the sailors will not believe it."

"I can hardly hoist it in, sir!"

"Hoist it in! It would carry away a dozen luff-tackles to hoist it in."

"How thin her husband is, sir!"

"Thin! He may get under the lee of a rope-yarn."

"I think, sir, that already the old man is jealous of you."

"As surely as the *Desdemona* is now going through the water. Why, when I took his wife by the hand, he looked at me marlinespikes."

"He changed colour in the face, sir, like a dolphin."

"Come, Hurricane, drink your wine. Here's to the wind that blows, the ship that goes, and the lass that loves a sailor."

Here the conversation was interrupted by the entrance of Flora, who came down under the pretence of finding her smelling-bottle.

The captain and lieutenant rose to receive her.

"Captain!" exclaimed Flora; "do you know I have lost my

smelling-bottle, and Mr Factor is angry with me for it."

"Angry with such loveliness!" exclaimed captain Brilliant. "Good God!"

Flora had insensibly taken a seat next the captain, who was caressing her fine form. The lieutenant expressed an apprehension that he was wanted upon deck, and withdrew from the cabin.

"Lord," said Flora, "what did that man make his exit so quick for?"

"He is gone upon deck, my dear, to keep a look-out a-head for squalls."

"Squalls! Captain! By goles, if I don't go up myself directly, I know Mr Factor will be squalling out after me."

"You have sweet lips, Flora. Notwithstanding my love of fighting, I would rather engage them, than an enemy's frigate."

"For shame! Captain!" said Flora.

"Another pull!" cried captain Brilliant.

"My dear Brilliant!" said Flora.

"A long pull, Flora, a strong pull, and a pull both together."

"For shame! captain!" exclaimed the lady.

"Flora! I say, Flora!" cried Mr Factor, poking his head down the ladder; while the lieutenants and midshipmen were giggling upon deck. "Flora! I say, Flora! It takes you a long time to look for your smelling-bottle."

"Unhand me! captain, I beseech you," cried Flora. "Don't you hear my husband? I am coming, my dear: I am only getting a handkerchief out of the trunk, to tie round your neck. I'm afraid, love, you will catch cold, by being exposed to the wind."

Flora now ascended the ladder, followed by captain Brilliant, who bowing to Mr Factor, expressed a hope he would not catch cold in his head; and told the lieutenant of the watch to take another reef in the topsails.

The topsail-yards were now lowered down: the reef-tackles were hauled out; and the lieutenant having exclaimed, "Away, aloft there!" the topmen scrambled up the rigging with the agility of monkeys, and lying out upon the yards, soon busied themselves in reducing the sails of the ship; while the midshipman on each cap, vociferated to the people, "Light out there! to windward! Light out, men, cheerly!"

Chapter 4

THERE being no ship visible, and the cruise of the *Desdemona* having expired, captain Brilliant shaped his course for Spithead, where he found Mr Echo arrived with the prize.

And now, the bosom of Flora rose with emotion, at the thought of separating from captain Brilliant and his officers. She gave a world of sighs, and could scarce repress the tear that trembled in her eye. But Mr Factor hurried her into the boat; and she waved her hand to captain Brilliant, who stood kissing his own to her on the gangway.

"She's gone!" exclaimed captain Brilliant, to the first lieutenant. "The old fellow has shoved his boat off! What an infernal splice! What a damnable sacrifice!"

"And yet, sir," said Mr Hurricane, "she vowed before the chaplain, at the altar, to love, honor, and obey her husband, till death cut away the life-lines of either one or the other."

"She might tell the parson so," cried captain Brilliant; "but I'll be d—d if the sailors will believe it."

It being necessary to overhaul the *Desdemona's* rigging, captain Brilliant hired horses, and, accompanied by his steward, proceeded into Wales.

Was the hero of this tale, then, a descendant from Caractacus, that he betook himself into Wales? Or was he drawn thither by some Cambrian damsel, fair as the snow that covers the mountains? A little patience, courteous reader, and your curiosity shall be relieved.

About a mile from Caerfilly, dwelled an aged admiral, who having done with the fatigues of a maritime life, enjoyed both ease and dignity in retirement; and centered his happiness in the education of a niece, who loved and venerated him with the tenderness of a child.

Cassandra Temple had scarcely seen more than seventeen summers. She was not, perhaps what is termed a regular beauty; but her eyes were dark and sparkling; her form was unobjectionable; and it was impossible to behold in any maid a finer bosom, a more elegant arm, or a neater foot.

The admiral, her uncle, kept much company; and a thousand beaux had whispered soft nonsense into the ear of Cassandra; but it never reached her heart; and, in fact, it may be said, she did not know she had a heart, till she saw captain Brilliant.

For six months she had now, however, experienced the heart-ache: and every time the wind blew, she sighed for her absent sailor.

Admiral Roughnot received the papers regularly from London,

and he always made it a practice to read the naval intelligence aloud. Her alighted one day on a paragraph, that made the little heart of Cassandra go pit-a-pat.

"Yesterday morning, the *Desdemona,* captain Brilliant, arrived at Spithead."

"Captain Brilliant," said the old man: "is not that, Cassandra, the youth who dined with us one day, when sir Hugh Morgan paid us a visit, with his children and grandchildren? I remember the day particularly, for you were taken ill a short time after their departure."

"Yes, uncle," sighed Cassandra; "and I too, remember the day."

"You were very ill, Cassandra."

"Yes, uncle, indeed; I was ill in my heart."

"He was a likely young fellow," added the old man.

Cassandra sighed.

"He was very officer-like in his manners," continued the admiral.

Cassandra repeated her sigh.

"Those long shore men, sir Hugh's sons, could not hold a light to him where he came. The eyes of Miss Morgan seemed clinched upon the captain."

In this manner the admiral went on, for an hour, to indulge his garrulity; nor could he have selected a more interesting theme for Cassandra, who listened to her uncle with tumultuous rapture.

Captain Brilliant rode into Wales, actuated apparently by no other motive than to see his friend, sir Hugh Morgan; but the real object of his journey was to obtain an interview with Cassandra, who dwelt within a mile of the baronet's seat.

Sir Hugh and his sons received our hero with transports. "Tantivy!" cried the baronet. "Tantivity! tantivy!"—The whole family crouded round him: the fatted calf was killed; and all was joy, mirth, and jubilee.

Brilliant cursed, in secret, the importunities of the family; and it was not till twilight that he could escape from the hall. The moon was rising, and, guided by its light, he directed his steps to the dwelling of Cassandra.

It was a summer's evening, and Cassandra was sitting at a window that looked into the garden, in maiden meditation, fancy free! She was repeating a favorite stanza of a poem, when captain Brilliant approached.

Lovely seems the moon's full glory,
To the fainting seaman's eyes,
When some horrid storm dispersing,
O'er the waves her radiance flies.

Here Cassandra gave a sigh, which seemed to exhale her soul through her lips, and then gave vent to her feelings in the following soliloquy:

"My lover has passed many seas; he has wandered to distant shores. At this moment the prow of his vessel is cleaving the deep. Oh! when the wind blows in wrath, and rouses the surges from their sleep, it is then I sigh for the safety of my sailor; it is then my fancy magnifies the dangers that encompass him.

"I now from my window behold the waves spend their rage on the shore. The cottager hears it, and rejoices in his safety. It is my sailor who is exposed to danger. In vain does the sigh of love distend my bosom. It is lost in the blast. In vain do my eyes roll in sorrow o'er the deep. The bark of my lover mounts not on the waves!"

Thus spoke Cassandra; her hair falling in sweet disorder over her well-turned shoulders, and her white arm supporting her leaning cheek.

"It is now near night," resumed the maid, "but, sailor of my heart! shall I taste the joys of sleep, when thou art exposed to danger? Oh! dost thou ever think of me in the season of dreams? Is my image ever seen in thy slumbers of the night?"—

"Yes! my sea-goddess!" exclaimed Brilliant,—"every night; lying in my cot, I fancy I see thee, that I hold thee in my arms! My dream is now realized! I now feel thee in my embrace; feel the beat of thy bosom, the warmth of thy lips!"

The window of Cassandra's summer-house was low. She yielded to the impassioned embrace of her lover. She reclined her head on his breast. She listened to the accents of his voice in silence. The heaving of her white bosom met his heart. Her roseat lips were pressed by the son of the ocean. Sighs from both were intermingled, and love fled from eye to eye.

"Oh! Brilliant!" cried Cassandra, with a faultering voice. "May we meet again never to be separated by the ocean!"

"No never! I come to take you with me to sea."

"Oh! I will go with you round the world."

Here the tender discourse of these fond lovers was interrupted by the sound of a horn, and the cry of "Stole away! stole away!" which was vociferated from the lungs of sir Hugh Morgan, and which echo repeated from every hill and every dale.

"D—n that fellow!" exclaimed the captain; "he has got his broth, and is come in pursuite. Cassandra, I must shove my boat off, or our interview will be discovered."

"Good night! Good night!" cried Cassandra, meeting, rather than repulsing the embrace of the captain.

Captain Brilliant now took to his heels; and, for the first time in his life, might have been said to have run away. He leaped hedges, and ditches, and gates, and fences; till, by a circuitous route, he reached the house of the baronet, without affording any clue to trace his nightly pilgrimage.

The baronet beat up the quarters of the admiral, and earnestly inquired for his kindsman. The noble sea-officer denied having seen him, but expressed his hope that the captain was in health.

"Tantivy! Tantivy!" bellowed the baronet. "Hark away! Hark away!" And so saying, he danced back to his house, followed by all his dogs, in full cry.

The captain devised an excuse, which satisfied sir Hugh.

"Finding it devilish hot," said the captain, "I went to bathe myself in your pond: and I now return to you with a double flow of spirits."

"Bathe in my pond!" cried sir Hugh. "You shall bathe in a bowl of grog. I would rather see you than the great mogul. You shall drink till you cannot see out of your eyes. Here's success to the *Desdemona*! I know you will fight, my boy; I know you will kill every enemy to our king, our constitution, and our religion. Yard-arm and yard-arm! chain-shot and grape-shot. Single-round and double-round! Cartridges and wads! Shoot away! my brave boys! You trespass on no manor. The sea knows no gamekeepers. Fire away, my brave boys! Hearts of oak! Wooden walls! Rule Britannia!"

And here I conclude the chapter; acquainting my reader, upon the veracity of an historian, that, however stupidly intoxicated sir Hugh became before midnight, our hero did not degrade himself below a beast but retired to bed sober.

Chapter 5

THE conference of the lovers being interrupted by the clamours of the intoxicated baronet, Cassandra had not been allowed time to acquaint the captain that a titled rival had professed himself her devoted humble servant; and was encouraged by the admiral to prosecute his suite.

This rival was lord Fiddlefaddle, a youth of immense fortune, but who had been spoiled by the indulgence of his mother. Valuable individuals are scarce, and it was a duty his lordship owed his country to take care of himself. He wore chicken-skin gloves; encased his body with stays, and when he washed his hands had recourse always to rose-water.

The following day, captain Brilliant was invited, with sir Hugh and his family, to dine at the admiral's; where lord Fiddlefaddle had got before them, and was whispering tender things to Cassandra, when the guests entered the room.

"My lord," said the admiral, "allow me to introduce captain Brilliant to you."

"I am," cried lord fiddlefaddle, "captain Brilliant's most obedient and very humble servant. Cass, my fair bride, it is not, I think, in my power to be more obedient or more humble,"—And so saying, his lordship took an opera-glass from his pocket, and began to reconnoitre the captain.

"And I, sir," said captain Brilliant, "am lord Fiddlefaddle's most humble-come-tumble out of the maintop into the lower-hold!—I would not wish to fall further."

"Technical!" exclaimed his lordship.—"Cassandra, tell me, my bride! are you of the same opinion as the countess dowager of Fitz-Quizzerie: She says I have a nose exactly like Julius Caesar's?"

This was too much for the risible muscles of Brilliant. He laughed till he roared: not more tremendous was the roar of Homer's gods united. But not wishing to transgress the rules of good-breeding, he was about to prefer an excuse, when perceiving lord Fiddlefaddle draw his sword half way out of the scabbard, his laughter redoubled.

"Let me come at him!" exclaimed his lordship, "I will impale him with my sword!"

"Murder!" cried the captain. "Help, here! or I shall be slain!"

The company now interposed their offices of peacemaking; sir Hugh repressed the arm of the valorous peer, and the admiral restrained the laughter of the side-shaking captain.

"Next mind," said his lordship: "I will put up my sword in the presence of women; but I shall find time and place. Death before dishonor."

"His lordship looks big," whispered the eldest Morgan in the ear of the captain. "See how he struts!"

"He now walks the deck," said the captain, "as stiff as a midshipman; but a single lee-lurch of the *Desdemona* would shake him to oakum."

Dinner was now served up. Cassandra did the honors of the table. She looked extremely dejected, for she was not only annoyed by the pestilential compliments of lord Fiddlefaddle, but she witnessed that the melting eye of miss Morgan was perpetually directing its artillery at the captain.

Dinner ended, the ladies withdrew, followed by lord Fiddlefaddle, who vowed it was a barbarous John-Bull custom, to sit soaking over a bottle, and leave the women to pine, like so many turtles for their mates.

The wine was therefore circulated among those who had heads to bear it; and it was not till the gentlemen had respectively drank a couple of bottles, that they ascended to the drawing-room.

Lord Fiddlefaddle had drawn his chair close to Cassandra, who was biting her lips with vexation to be so pestered by a popinjay. He was relating to her the movements of the Caerfilly volunteers, whom he had reviewed the preceding day. "Our fatigues," said he, "were, without any hyperbole, not exceeded by Hannibal, when he crossed the Alps. We marched and counter-marched, at least a dozen miles. There was no intermission to our toil. Should the French ever have the temerity to invade us, they will find veterans to oppose."

Captain Brilliant approached the eldest miss Morgan: it was but common politeness, for there was an unoccupied chair by her side.

"How enviable are your military men," whispered Brilliant: "what power a red coat has over the hearts of the fair. Only observe how miss Cassandra sighs when his lordship addresses her."

"She does indeed," said miss Morgan.

"I am sure," resumed the captain, "they must be soft as the breezes of the equator, or the hull of his lordship could never withstand them."

Miss Morgan could scarcely repress the impulse she felt to laugh, when the party was broken up by the movements of lord Fiddlefaddle, who, looking at his watch swore he had exceeded the hour of his promised visit to the countess dowager Fitz-Quizzerie;

and his coach being called, he left the house with as many bows as a French dancing-master.

None of my readers can be so dull as not to imagine that the hero and heroine of this tale were solicitous in their hearts once more to obtain an interview.

Love delights in the stillness of the night; and when Phoebe mounted her silver car, Cassandra repaired to her room, and reclined her cheek upon her hand, somewhat after the manner of Juliet in the play. She had been reading Shakespeare, and the scene before her associated one of his descriptions in her mind.

"O! beautiful night!" said Cassandra. "The moon lends her light to the footsteps of my lover."

"Yes!" cried the captain, faithful to his assignation: "here I come, Cassandra, like seven bells half struck."

"Welcome!" exclaimed Cassandra; "welcome to my eyes! How fair is the night!"

"But how much fairer you!" rejoined the captain. "How pretty your white robe shakes a cloth to the wind. Cassandra," added he, "you did not tell me I had a rival."

"He was not worthy to be mentioned."

"But he is a lord; and your uncle swears that you shall marry him."

"Alas! it is too true."

"And the rumour of the place is, that Thursday is the day appointed for you to be spliced."

"Alas! I know it."

"But reflect, Cassandra; thrice will the moon hide her head in the ocean before the day arrives; and on the preceding night, guided by its friendly beams, shove your boat off with me."

"Heigho! My heart beats strangely."

"I have already procured a license from a chaplain, and engaged a chaise and four. So all now wanting is your consent; and then we will be spliced."

"But, provided I become your wife, will you, my dear Brilliant, take me with you to sea? It would break the heart of poor Cassandra to be separated by the wide ocean from the husband of her election."

"Bravo! my pretty sailor. You shall grace the cabin of the *Desdemona.* An accommodation ladder shall be prepared for the lady of the captain; the boatswain shall attend the side, and the marines be drawn up to receive you."

"Then on Wednesday I will be your's, if you will have poor Cassandra."

"Yes! Cassandra, and I will so prize the gift, that I would not exchange you for all the pearls, gold and silver, in Davy Jones's locker."

Chapter 6

I REMEMBER once having been told by a young lady, who had eloped to be married, that a woman in such a situation never goes off unprovided with a bundle. Whether it be, that a woman's love of dress never forsakes her; or, that she looks to maintaining the conquest her beauty has achieved, by the adventitious aid of the milliner and mantua-maker.

When captain Brilliant came to the window to Cassandra, at the appointed hour, she had not only dressed in an appropriate manner to elope, but had made up a little bundle of clothes to accompany her.

The admiral was now out, and Brilliant was admitted to her room by Prudence, her faithful servant and confidant, who was ready to partake of the fortunes of her mistress.

"Oh, Brilliant!" cried Cassandra, "how I tremble! My hand shakes so, that I am utterly incapable of writing a note to my uncle."

"Give me the pen, my dear," said Brilliant; "I will write the admiral a note ship-shape."

Captain Brilliant took the pen, and wrote as follows:

Sir,

Your niece being a lass who loves a sailor, declines the marriage settlement of my lord Fiddlefumble, to be spliced to a man who has no other house but his ship; which will sufficiently explain the motive of her shoving her boat off.

I have the honour to be, etc.

BRYAN BRILLIANT.

The every-day writers of tales have an invariable custom of making their lovers elope at the conclusion of their histories; but, disdaining such rules, behold the hero and heroine of this page running away in the middle of my eventful story; or, in language more correct, run away with by four blood horses, and pursuing their course to the New Ferry Passage. Yes! let the reader picture to his imagination Cassandra, Prudence and the captain sitting in a comfortable chaise, and gallopping, hurry-skurry, to the altar of Hymen.

Captain Brilliant was married to Cassandra at Bristol: and it would require language superior to that of mortals to paint the bliss of Captain Brilliant, when he found himself in the arms of his beloved Cassandra. It has been said by the poet that *man never is, but always to be blest.* Pope deceived himself; for Brilliant was supremely blest in the possession of so much loveliness. And had Pope tasted the happiness of the married state, he never would have advanced such a position.

Chapter 7

THOUGH the last chapter may be found short, it was still very eventful; and it now remains for me to relate that captain Brilliant proceeded with his lady to Portsmouth, where his orders had fortunately arrived only an hour before.

"Bravo!" cried the captain to his wife. "Every thing smiles upon our union. Touch and go is a good pilot."

"But when do you go on board?"

"The moment you are ready."

"I am ready now," said Cassandra, throwing her arms round his neck.

"Well then, my love," cried the captain, "I will write a note to my first lieutenant, to get the whip ready for you."

"My dear Brilliant!" said Cassandra:—"surely you are not a Russian. What have I done to deserve the whip?"

Here the captain laughed heartily, (as I humbly trust my readers will do) when, having explained himself to Cassandra, he wrote his first lieutenant a note.

Dear Hurricane,

Get the whip ready. I am spliced.

Your's,

BRYAN BRILLIANT.

The coxswain of the barge returned with the following answer.

Dear Sir,

So am I! and a devil of a splice I have made.

I have the honour to be, etc.

HENRY HURRICANE.

Captain Brilliant having dined with Cassandra, at the hotel on the Point, and introduced his bride to lord Fearless, sir Joshua Invincible, and the honourable captain Cutwater, who commanded ships lying in the harbour, he embarked with Cassandra and Prudence, and a French lap-dog, in the barge, and was conveyed on board the *Desdemona.*

But, on ascending the ship's side, our noble captain could not repress his astonishment at the uproar that prevailed on the quater-deck of the frigate.

There was a young woman leaning against the capstern, stamping her cap under foot, and upbraiding the first lieutenant with every opprobrious epithet that an enraged woman could utter.

"You deceitful man!" cried the lady. "Was it for this I married you before my last husband was laid in his grave, and put you in possession of a bag full of joes? Shame on you, you low fellow! To descend to a strumpet, when you had a wife on board your ship."

"Indeed Flora, you are wrong."

"What! have I not the use of my eyes, that you thus exculpate your conduct. Did I not see the woman take you by the arm. Did you not smile on her? Ha! you thought I was snug on board, and ignorant of your villany. But I suspected your conduct. Put me, I say, ashore! I will not stay another moment on board."

"Avast there! Flora. The boats are all hoisted in. We have got our sailing orders on board. The fore-topsail is loose. Captain Brilliant is come. I must get the ship under weigh."

Cassandra and Prudence were now hoisted on board; and the former was melted into tenderness on beholding the distraction of a young and beautiful girl.

"What, my dear," said she to her husband, "is the matter?"

"Faith," cried the captain, "here is the devil to pay, and no pitch hot. I think I have had the pleasure of seeing that lady before. Mrs Factor, if I mistake not?"

"Yes, sir," sobbed the lady: "my name was Factor. You, not long ago, had the goodness to take me and my husband into your ship. You remember the morning I left you; Mr Factor died the same night, of convulsions, in his bed. Not knowing a soul at Portsmouth, I returned on board the ship, and wanted to see you; hoping you could recommend me to some lady to lodge with. You was gone to your friends; but your first lieutenant received me: and when I told him my tale, he affected to feel for me; beseeched me not to afflict myself, and immediately accompanied me to Mrs Read, who accommodated me with a first floor on the Point. At that time, sir, I had no more thought of him, than I have now of you; and I was not a little surprised to receive from him a letter. I will read it to you."

"Avast there!" cried the lieutenant. "Avast, and spare my blushes."

"This is the letter, sir," said Flora.

Divine Flora,

The havoc committed by shells thrown into the seaport of an enemy, is a mere trifle in war-time, compared, queen of queens! to the destruction of my heart from the fire of your eyes. Yes! goddess of goddesses! a shot from either one or both of those heavenly bow-chasers has raked my heart fore and aft and knocked it into splinters; splinters that no carpenter can repair but the magic of your smiles. Alack! alack! every time I lie down in my hammock, I fairly make the clues strand, conceiting I hold you, beautiful Flora, in my arms: and if this be not a proof of my most ardent love, I know not in which point of the compass it lies. Lowering my top-gallant-sails to you.

I am your dying lieutenant,
HENRY HURRICANE.

To be grave, on hearing this letter read, exceeded all power of face. "Ha! ha! ha!" roared the captain. "Bravo! Hurricane! By the piper that played before Moses in the woods, you went upon the right tack. Ah! let a sailor alone for laying an anchor out to windward of a fair lady."

"Well, sir," continued Mrs Factor, "the next morning he came ashore in a full suit of uniform, a gold laced hat, and a swaggering sword by his side; and being admitted to my presence, threw himself at my feet. He swore I was more beautiful in my undress (I was in *dishabille*) than a seventy-four gun ship in full sail; and after heaping a thousand praises on what he called my top-lights: he implored I would suffer him to send for a chaplain to splice us together. At first I could with difficulty repress my smiles; but when I saw the man take his handkerchief from his pocket and cry like a schoo-boy,"—

"I beg pardon for interrupting you, madam," said the captain, "but I suspect Mr Hurricane had an onion in his pocket."

"Upon my soul, sir," answered the lieutenant, "when I thought she scorned my passion, I wept like a child."

"Belay there!" cried the captain; "you may tell that to the marines, but I'll be d—d if the sailors will believe it."

"Well, sir," resumed Flora, "beholding a man weep for me, who I knew but a few days before, was burning with impatience, to encounter the enemies of his country, my heart was melted into tenderness, and I consented to become his wife. We were married privately the next day; and I will candidly acknowledge that the ardour of a young officer soothed into oblivion the memory of my old merchant."

"Yes, Flora," interrupted the lieutenant, "you found me no *Plato-comic* lover."

"Well, captain," continued Flora, "I now thought myself happy; and I put into the hands of my new husband a bag full of joes, I also accompanied him on board the frigate, and I loved him so in my heart, that I would have gone with him, cheerfully, in a voyage round the world. But I soon found my happiness vanish like a dream. My husband pretended that he had business at the dock-yard, and desired I would amuse myself with a book till he returned. But suspecting that, in reality, he was tired of my company, I followed in another boat, and popped upon my *dying lieutenant* at the door of a bad house, toying, in the company of some more lieutenants, with several vulgar wenches, whose bold looks would have disgusted a man of the least sentiment."

"Hurricane," said the captain, "here is a grand charge against you. Were you to be tried by a court-martial, where there were a jury of husbands, you would certainly be transferred to the bottom of Hymen's list."

"Indeed, sir," said the lieutenant, "I am an innocent fellow."—"Yes," rejoined the captain, "so it appears."

"Why, sir," said the lieutenant, "the fact was this: Having dined at the blue-posts, with three or four of my old messmates; in walking down together to the boat at the Point, we passed a house where there were half a dozen young women before the door. They all of them hailed us: but all I wanted was to luff up, to bear away to keep clear of the fleet; for I had now got a wife, and had entirely done with drifting. But I was embarrassed in the clinch. For just as I was endeavouring to shove off my boat from them, a girl lays hold of me stock and flucke, and swears I shall not leave her."

"Yes," cried Flora, "she hanged and lolled upon you; and you smiled, and was ready to accompany her into the house."

"How now," rejoined the lieutenant, "I was trying to get from the house, and had already cleared myself from the arms of the woman, when lo! my wife appears, and reads the articles of war to me."

"Well," said the captain, "we will hoist the barge in upon the strength of it."

The yard and stay-tackles of the frigate were now hauled down, and hooked to the barge; the falls were manned, and the boatswain, together with his three mates, began to tune

> the shrill whistle, which doth order give
> To sounds confus'd.

The sailors were making a run of the tackle-falls, and Mr Hurricane, the lieutenant, was heard to exclaim, "Silence there! Step out, men! step out! Walk away with him, cheerly!"

In one minute the barge was suspended in the air, between the main and fore-yards. And now were heard the following orders, which had the magic to place the boat upon the booms:—

"High enough with the stays. Avast there! Lower away the yards! Lower away the stays! Let go!"

Chapter 8

THE orders, which I have observed, captain Brilliant had received from the secretary of the admiralty, commanded him to proceed without delay, to the coast of America, and cruise for three months off the Capes of Virginia.

The *Desdemona* had already taken on board provisions for half a year, and she was otherwise equipped for an absence from England.

The topsails were, therefore, sheeted home and hoisted; the capstern bars were again manned; the anchor the ship rode at, was hove up to the bows; and, being cast by lieutenant Hurricane, the frigate stood out of Spithead with solemn majesty of mien.

Hotspur exclaimed to his wife, "Kate, you shall see me ride!" But Hurricane might have said to his wife, "Flora, you shall see me get a ship underweigh!"

The sails being trimmed, captain Brilliant descended with the blooming Cassandra, and saluting her, cried, "Welcome, my sweet love, on board the ship I command. But, alas! I am apprehensive you will soon wish yourself in Wales, where you were under no fear of bringing your anchors home."

"Indeed my love," said Cassandra, "your suspicions are unjust. The shore and the sea are alike to Cassandra, provided she is with you."

"You will not," returned the captain, "be without the society of your sex. Though Mrs Hurricane is somewhat violent, her manners still discover elegance and ease."

"She is indeed," said Cassandra, "a very pretty young woman. I pray you, invite her below."

"Prudence," said the captain, "acquaint Mrs Hurricane we are going to tea. Oh! you are nursing monsieur *Bijou*: all the chicken bones shall be saved for him."

Mrs Hurricane descended into the cabin, more composed in her aspect.

"My dear madam," said she to Cassandra, "I hope you will excuse my impetuosity; but I love my husband so violently, that it made me quite forget myself. Lord! how he contrives to make the ship gallop along with us. Are you not alarmed? And he roars so through his trumpet, that he would deafen a ballad-singer."

"Your husband, madam," cried captain Brilliant, "has got a top-chain down his throat. He is a noble sea officer. I know him on every tack. He was once a midshipman under me, and has risen to his present dignity by his zeal for the service. A better officer never took a speaking trumpet in his hand. If he has any fault, it is, that there is not a fine girl at the Point whom he has not had in tow."

"My dear Brilliant," said Cassandra, "forbear your strictures. Mrs Hurricane you must not mind my husband; he is only in jest."

"Ah!" sighed Mrs Hurricane, "I believe many a true word is said in jest. I know Hurricane made the first overture to the wench I caught him with—I know the inconstant did! I will never have done rating him till I get at the truth."

Mr Hurricane here came down to confer with the captain. "It looks black, sir, to windward," said he; "shall we take another reef in the topsails?"

"Black!" repeated Flora, disdainfully. "Then it corresponds with your heart."

"Close-reef the pudding-bags, Mr Hurricane," replied the captain. "Take in the top-gallant-sails, and turn the hands up to reef the topsails."

Mr Hurricane had scarcely left the cabin, when the flag-ship at Spithead fired her evening gun.

"There," said captain Brilliant, "goes the commodore down the main hatchway."

And now the party sat down to enjoy their tea in the cabin, over which much pleasantry and good humour prevailed. The steward, together with the captain's servant, waited at table; and the sail-maker was busily employed in one corner, putting a new pair of clues to the captain's cot.

"Let my geer be strong," said the captain to the sail-maker, "for I expect we shall have some hard squalls in the night. Mrs Hurricane, how are you, madam? Do you feel a little sick at stomach?"

"A little, sir."

"Ha, Hurricane, I perceive, has already laid the keel of a young one."

The ship's bell having rung for eight o'clock, lieutenant Taffarel went upon deck to relieve lieutenant Hurricane; when, exchanging a man-of-war's bow, they fell together into the quarter-deck step, and conversed with much gaiety.

"Why! damn it, Hurricane," cried Taffarel, "the captain and you have both gone upon the same tack, and both fetched the same port. His wife is a beauty. But what is it he calls her? Cat-fall-andra? 'Tis a very good name, for she has a noble pair of cat-heads."

"She seems," said Hurricane, "to be a nice sea-boat. But as to mine, she'll neither stay, nor wear, nor lie-too, nor scud."

"Psha!" said Taffarel, "you don't know her trim yet."

"What a passion," cried Hurricane, "she was in this afternoon, when the captain came along-side. By ——! I was ashamed of myself. The ship is no better than a privateer."

"She looked very warlike," said Taffarel. "I thought more than once, she would have flattened your jib-sheet in."

"It cannot be helped," retored Hurricane, "hard up and she cracks."

"Have you heard the news?" said Taffarel.

"What is it?" cried Hurricane.

"Why, the third lieutenant is on the doctor's list; and you and I, this night, must keep watch and watch."

"It is the same thing to me. The middle watch is mine. It is you who will have two skulks in the lee-scuppers."

"Damn all watches! I would sell mine to any body for a trifle."

"'Tis the fortune of war."

"Where's your wife, Hurricane?"

"She is in the main-top, picking gooseberries."

"You would not let her go ashore!"

"Yes, I would, if she would have gone upon the sheet anchor."

"Ha, ha! that would be next to heaving her over the standing part of the main-sheet."

"What did you think of the letter?"

"It was sublime, by heaven! When Flora read it, I knew it was your's. I knew your hand writing."

"I did not think she would overhaul it again. How the captain laughed!"

"Laughed! It made all hands laugh. 'Your dying lieutenant!' That was much better than dying swain, for what is a long-shore-man compared to a sailor."

"Well, I must go below. I get no more rest than the vane at the mast-head. Taffarel! take care the ship does not fall over-board."

"Aye aye, sir! aye, aye! But Mr Hurricane, hark you, you have not told me which way the ship's head is?"

"Her head is between the two cat-heads."

"Well bear a-hand, and get your anchor a cock-bill."

"It already hangs by the stopper. My shank-painter is let go; and I have roused up a good range of cable upon deck."

"Then, let go the anchor!"

Chapter 9

LIEUTENANT HURRICANE, having gone below, dispatched the gun-room steward into the cabin, with his compliments to Mrs Hurricane, and he was going to turn in.

"Carry the message ashore," said Mrs Hurricane; "he does not want me."

"Indeed, madam, he does," returned the steward. "Your husband is now walking up and down the gunroom with his hands in his beckets."

"Ha! ha!" laughed the captain.

Waiting for th' appointed minute,
  Oft he paces to and fro;
Stopping now—now moving forwards,
  Sometimes quick and sometimes slow.

"Shall I say, madam," cried the steward, "that you are coming?"

"No! I am not married to a fore-mast-man. I will not go to bed at eight o'clock. Such an hour only suits the vulgar."

"It is almost nine, madam: Mr Hurricane waited for you till one bell."

"Ha! ha!" laughed the captain again.

Softly blow the evening breezes,
  Softly fall the dews of night;
Yonder walks my first lieutenant,
  Shunning every glare of light!

"Mr Hurricane," cried the steward, "says he cannot, madam, sleep without you."

"His wife," said Flora, "will not believe that."

"Nor the sailors either," rejoined the captain; "it will only do for the marines."

"Go, my dear girl," said Cassandra.

"Will you come, madam?" asked the steward.

"Let my husband come and attend me," said Flora.

"Yes," rejoined the captain; "tell Mr Hurricane to come and convoy his wife down the ladder."

"Aye! aye! sir;" cried the steward.

In a few minutes lieutenant Hurricane made his appearance, with a lanthorn in his hand. "My dear," said he, "you are very slack in stays."

"Slack in stays!" said Flora. "I have no stays on. Go to your wenches, you low fellow."

"Handsomely! handsomely, Flora," cried the lieutenant. "You forget, that in a short time you will be out of soundings. You forget, madam, that soon I shall have you in blue water."

"Go to the dock again," replied Flora.

"I want to get you into dock," said the lieutenant. "Come! do heave up your anchors. You know, my dear, what a long time it takes you to undress. You are as long rigging and unrigging as a seventy-four gun ship."

"Surprising!" said the captain. "Now, my wife will strip ship in a minute."

"My dear Brilliant!" said Cassandra.

"Pray, Flora, spring your luff," said the lieutenant. "It takes you half an hour to get on your shifting-backstay-nightcap."

"Good-night, Mrs Brilliant," said Flora.

"Good-night, my dear," replied Cassandra.

"Good-night, Mrs Hurricane," said the captain. "Mind you square the yards by the lifts and braces. Hurricane! I suspect we shall have to send down top-gallant yards. There will be some hard squalls before the morning."

The steward now got out the cot, and our hero went up the ladder with his lady.

When captain Brilliant came upon deck with Cassandra, a more beautiful scene could scarcely be imagined than that which presented itself. The moon was gazing at her face in the water, the sails were reflected on the deep, and the repose of the night was disturbed only by the roar of the ocean, whose talking waves the sea-boy child as he lolled over the bow.

The bell was now struck four; the man at the wheel was relieved, and the log was hove.

"She goes eleven knots, sir," said the master's mate, addressing the lieutenant with a bowing mien.

"Ha!" cried the captain, "she walks through it indeed."

"What is a knot?" said Cassandra.

"A knot, my love," replied the captain, "is a mile."

"How loud it blows," said Cassandra.

"Yes, my dear," said the captain: "the wind whistles through the blocks, as the old fellow observed, when he had only half a sheave at his mast-head."

"Does it ever blow harder at sea?" said Cassandra.

"Harder! my dear," replied the captain. "It sometimes blows hard enough to blow the devil's horns off."

"My dear Brilliant!" said Cassandra.

"Cassandra," whispered the captain, "it is too cold for you to be upon deck. Come below and turn in."

"Let me stay upon deck a little longer," said Cassandra. "The sea is so awful. It reminds me of a passage in the Bible. *They that go down to the sea in ships, that do business in great waters; these see the works of the Lord, and his wonders in the deep!*"

"Then you read the Bible sometimes," said the captain.

"Yes, my dear," replied Cassandra. "It always makes me cheerful."

"And do you believe about Jonas and the whale?" said the captain. "That will only do for the marines."

"Indeed," retorted Cassandra, "I believe it from my heart. What may not be effected by supernatural interposition?"

"Mr Taffarel!" cried the captain, "the wind is coming aft. Haul in the weather-braces."

"Send the after-guard and marines aft, here!" exclaimed the lieutenant, "to the weather-mainbrace! Up there! a blue jacket! and bear those backstays abreast the top-brim. Where are the main-top-men? Boatswain's mate! start the main-top-men aft here. Haul in the main-brace! Pull together, men! Mind the weather-roll! There you are well with the main-yard! Tie him there! Tie him there! Don't come up any! Belay every inch of that!"

The other yards were now squared in succession, by the watch; and the *Desdemona* urged her course with glory through the wind-obeying deep. Time stole insensibly along; the log was again hove for midnight; the bell was rung, and the boatswain's mate was heard to pipe and exclaim thrice, "Starboard watch a-hoy! Star-bowlines ahoy."

The quarter-master now went below to call the midshipmen, of whom many being old men-of-war's men, stood two calls; and a midshipman descended to wake lieutenant Hurricane, who was snoring by the side of his wife.

"Curse all watching!" cried Hurricane, rising up in his bed. "I wish my mother had sold vinegar, and I had staid at home to bottle it off. I get no more rest than a dog-vane!"

"My dear," said Flora, "if you go upon deck, I will go with you." And so saying, she threw her arms round the neck of lieutenant Hurricane, with such blushing cheeks, that the lieutenant, like a true man-of-war's man, stood a second call before he turned out.

At length Mr Hurricane came up the companion-ladder, accompanied by Flora, who had wrapped herself up in her husband's great-coat.

"Ha! ha!" laughed the captain, "Who have we here! A friend of the baker or a friend of the brewer?"

"She is both, sir, I believe," said Mr Hurricane. "Here we come, sir, together! Here we come, sir, like a bunch of rope-yarns tied up in a granny's knots."

"My dear Flora!" said Cassandra, "what brought you up in the cold?"

"I cannot sleep by myself," replied Flora; "I come to keep watch with Hurricane."

"Bravo!" cried the captain: "you will soon be a sailor. You will soon be able to do your duty in any part of the ship."

"She can already, sir," said Hurricane, "both hand and steer."

"Was there not a heavy squall in the night?" said the captain.

"Yes, sir," returned the lieutenant. "My poor wife was taken aback; but she soon boxed her ship off."

"Come, Cassandra," said the captain, "let us descend and turn in. If I don't ease my laniard, I shall carry away my bob-stay."

"Good night, Mrs Hurricane," cried Cassandra; "I hope you will take no cold."

"Good night, madam," replied Flora; "I hope you will sleep well."

And now I shall conclude this chapter, leaving lieutenant Hurricane and his wife in charge of the quarter-deck, and His Majesty's frigate the *Desdemona*, going large before the wind, at the rate of thirteen knots and a half an hour.

Chapter 10

AN easterly wind prevailing, the *Desdemona* soon cleared the channel, and stood out to sea. For the first three or four days, the ladies were not without a few qualms at their stomachs; but their sickness subsided with the gale, and the roses returned to their dimpled faces.

It was off the Azores that captain Brilliant fell in with, and spoke an English seventy-four gun ship. The private signal being mutually answered, the two ships ranged up alongside of one another, and reciprocal inquiries passed between them.

"What frigate is that?" cried the captain of the seventy-four.

"The *Desdemona.*"

"The *Desdemona*! Then how is captain Brilliant?"

"Hearty, at your service. But I declare you have the advantage of me."

"What! have you forgot the voice of your messmate Tempest?"

"What, is it you, Tempest! How are you? What cheer, my old friend?"

"Hearty, hearty! How is your first lieutenant? Does he drift as much as ever among the girls?"

"Yes!" exclaimed Flora, "his character is notorious!"

"I have done with blowings, sir," said lieutenant Hurricane; "I am spliced. This lady, who now looks over the rough-tree-rail, has brought me up standing with a round turn double bitted. The chaplain at Portsmouth read a page to us out of Hamilton Moore."

"What the devil!" cried the strange captain, "another ship in tow? Why it was only three weeks ago that I saw the wife you married at Baltimore. I have a letter from her to you in my pocket. She is inconsolable for your departure. She missed stays just after you shoved off your boat. You had laid down the keel of a young luff."

"Great God!" exclaimed Flora, clasping her hands. "What do I hear! Take me! O! take me, sir, into your ship! Snatch me from the presence of the falsest of men!"

"Your eldest boy," resumed the strange captain, "is the very image of you. He grows rapidly. He is nearer heaven than he was by full half an inch."

"Heavenly God!" exclaimed Flora.

"Believe it not, Flora," said Mr Hurricane. "I was never married before. I have no son in the world. I am without an heir to my estates."

"Avast there!" replied captain Brilliant. "Heave and paul! You forget the child you had by Quassheba of Port Royal."

"Yes!" cried Flora; "your villany is confirmed. Take me from the ship! Take me from the ship! Oh! you deceiver!"

"Then go!" retorted lieutenant Hurricane. "Your behaviour is so unlike that ofan officer's lady, that the sooner you brace up and haul aft the better. Shall I hoist out the cutter, sir?"

"Yes, Mr Hurricane," replied the captain, "toss out the boat."

"Yes," said Flora, weeping, "you are all in a league against me. But I don't care. I'll go. And when I leave the ship, I will shake the dust off my feet."

"Hook on the cutter there!" said the lieutenant.

"Avast!" cried the captain. "Detain the cutter and expedite the barge."

"Barge-men away there!" cried a midshipman. "Coach-horses away there!" echoed the boatswain's mate. "All hands out barge! ahoy!"

"My dear girl," said Cassandra to Flora, "let not your suspicions triumph over your judgment. Sailors love to joke; and I would put no other construction upon what has been said. Be pacified by me, and do not mind what they say."

"You will never, madam," returned Flora, "convince me I am not deceived. You are not yet acquainted with the character of my husband. I will pack up my cloaths. I will go on board the other ship."

The boatswain and his mates now piped the hands up, to hoist out the barge.

"All hands!" exclaimed Mr Silvercall (having first piped) "out barge ahoy! Come, bear a-hand up there, men! Boatswain's mate!"—

"Sir!"

"Let me know who is last up the main hatchway."

"Aye, aye! sir! aye, aye!"

Both ships hove-to. It was nearly a calm: the ocean was unruffled; and the nymph-like form of Cassandra, who leaned over the quarter, was reflected from the deep.

The barge being hoisted out, captain Brilliant went on board the seventy-four, accompanied by Cassandra and Flora. Flora had made up a bundle of cloaths; and in descending the ship's side, gave no reply to lieutenant Hurricane, who had taken out his handkerchief and affected to weep.

The party was received with every elegance of urbanity by captain Tempest, of the *Salamander*: the cabin-doors were thrown open, and wine, and biscuit, together with the choicest tropical fruits, were placed on the table.

"Faith, Tempest," said Brilliant, "This is an excellent land-fall for the ladies."

The party having refreshed themselves, Cassandra, who had never before visited a line-of-battle ship, was shewn every part that could gratify curiosity. Nor was any attention omitted. The marines were under arms; the lieutenants had dressed themselves with studied elegance; and the midshipmen had pipe-clayed the weekly accounts to their collars.

At length a breeze sprang up; when it became necessary that the two ships should separate. The boat was ordered to be hauled up alongside. "*Desdemona's!* away, there!" vociferated the midshipman of the watch. "Call the sidesmen! Boatswain's-mate! tell Mr Stronglungs to attend the side!"

The visitors got ready to depart.

"Mrs Hurricane," said captain Brilliant, "allow me to assist you into the boat?"

"No, sir," replied Flora; "I will return to England. Captain Tempest will not, I dare say, refuse me a passage."

"But what will my first lieutenant," said captain Brilliant, "do for a wife?"

"He will find one where he is going," answered Flora.

"Do come," said Cassandra, "I entreat you."

"Indeed my dear, you must excuse me," returned Flora.

At this period, captain Tempest was reclining on his arm, and whispering tender things in the ear of Mrs Hurricane. Fragments of his discourse were overheard: "Better accommodations in this ship—the cabin more roomy—all things harmonious—unanimity and tranquility—officers polished—the yellow fever in America!"

"Come, Tempest," cried captain Brilliant, "don't be talking *sentimental* to Flora. Don't you be laying an anchor out to windward of my first lieutenant."

The *Desdemona* had now filled, and Mr Hurricane ranged up alongside of the seventy-four.

"*Desdemona!* ahoy!" cried captain Brilliant. "Hurricane!"

"Sir!" replied the lieutenant.

"Get your wife's chest and hammock ready to send on board here," cried captain Brilliant; "she is determined to draw the splice."

"Aye, aye! sir!" replied the lieutenant.

"Adieu, Flora! A pleasant passage back to your friends."

"Monster!" exclaimed Flora.

The barge now conveyed the captain and his lady back to the frigate, leaving Flora on board the seventy-four; who, however inflamed with indignation, could not repress a tear. But when the people reciprocally cheered on board the two ships, and each shaped a different course, the heart of Flora was ready to burst; it was then she bewailed the loss of her lieutenant; it was then she felt his value, which possession did not give her.

"Put me on board the *Desdemona*, I implore you! captain Tempest," cried Flora. "Restore me! oh! restore me to my best beloved Hurricane!"

"My sweet angel," said captain Tempest, "be not uneasy. You will soon forget your husband. These things are trifles in war-time."

"Oh! no! oh! no!" exclaimed Flora, "Stop the ship! oh! stop the ship!"

"By heaven!" said captain Tempest, "I must make a signal of distress. Get a gun ready on the forecastle!"

"All ready with the gun, sir!" cried the gunner.

"Fire away!"

The gun being fired, the seventy-four hauled up her courses, and backed her main-topsail, while the *Desdemona* hove in stays, and made a stretch under her quarter.

"*Desdemona!* ahoy!"

"Holloa!"

"My new passenger is distracted. She is crying for her lieutenant."

"Talk to her, Hurricane," said captain Brilliant.

"Flora!"

"My dear!"

"Then you don't like to sleep out of your hammock?"

"No, my dear!"

"Well then, I'll go on board for you.—Jolly-boat boys! away!"

The jolly-boat was lowered down from the davits abaft; lieutenant Hurricane went for his wife. Again the people cheered, and again the two ships separated.

The passage of the *Desdemona* across the Atlantic was pecualiarly favourable; and in a fortnight, after speaking the seventy-four, she made the Capes of Virginia, and sailed through those promontories, up the mighty bay of the Chesapeak.

The tide compelling them to let go an anchor, the ladies and officers went on shore in Gloucester Country. The corn-stalks bent under the clusters of the grain, and on this delicious food the party fed most luxuriously, enjoying, during their repast, the view of the frigate riding on the broad expanse of the bay.

The Virginians are hospitable. Their doors are always open to receive the stranger. Captain Brilliant and his lady, together with their friends, were invited to dine at the house of a Mr Keith. The adventures of this gentleman among the American Indians, were not a little celebrated, and he politely acquiesced with the desire of the captain to give him his history.

The wife, who had shared his dangers, was sitting by his side, when he thus began his narrative.

THE POST CAPTAIN

Chapter 11

The STORY OF Mr KEITH'S CAPTIVITY
among the AMERICAN INDIANS

IN the month of August 1795, I proceeded down the Ohio river, in a large boat, with a young wife, to whom I had been married a twelvemonth, and a child of three months old that she carried in her arms.

I was transporting my family and effects from Dog's Town to Fishing Creek, where I had purchased a mill, which stood hard by the Falls.

We felt some little regret on leaving our old abode. There is a certain attachment to place and thigs, by which a town, a house, or a tree, have an influence over the mind. Dog's Town is not an enviable place of residence; yet I doubt whether Baron Trenk left his dungeon without some degree of pensiveness.

Our feet clung to the threshold of the door of our old house. My wife gazed with wildness at the locust-tree, under whose shade she had so often sat with me, and listened to the mocking-bird's song: and I saw a tear fall from her eye upon the child that slept at her bosom.

A couple of negroes, Jack and Cuffey, rowed our canoe, and I undertook to steer her. Towards evening we had reached a broad part of the Ohio; the current ran strong in our favour; and there was less occasion for rowing, than to keep the canoe in the middle of the river.

The moon, in solemn majesty, was rising from the woods the fire-fly was on the wing, and the banks of the Ohio echoed with the incessant and melancholy cry of the whip-poor-will.

"Miss Keith!" cried the negro Cuffey, "something not aright. Something scare whip-poor-will. She cry like a mother that lose her pickniny."

I could not help smiling at the superstition of the fellow: but my wife drew nearer to me, and hugged the babe closer to her breast.

In a few minutes more, the most lamentable cries that ever were uttered assailed our ears. My wife screamed with affright, and the arms of the rowers were suspended.

I instantly put my fusil upon the whole cock, and kept the canoe in the middle of the stream, ordering at the same time the negroes to pull away.

I directed my eye towards the spot from whence the noise proceeded; and, being recovered from my emotion, could discern a white man kneeling on the bank of the river, supplicating me with every gesture and attitude that wretchedness could dictate, to take him into the boat.

I called to the men to lie upon their oars. The poor wretch repeated his cries. "Oh! take him on board!" exclaimed my wife; "his cries pierce my heart."

I steered towards the shore, and told the stranger to come on board.

"Alas!" faultered the man, "I have not strength left to move. For five days I have been without food, save now and then an acorn. Oh! leave me not to perish; but help me, I beseech you!"

I ordered the negroes to lift the man on board; but they had scarcely jumped on shore, when a dozen of indians rushed from a wood, yelling out the most diabolical screeches and notes and surrounded us in a twinkling.

The white man who had thus decoyed us a-shore was a prisoner to the Indians, and was employed by them, under the penalty of death, to ensnare the incautious passenger down the river, by his piercing cries and lamentable exclamations. Two captives they had dispatched with their war-clubs for refusing to perform the office.

I was quickly disarmed by the Indians, and Cuffey, in his attempt to flee into the woods, was overtaken by a young war-captain, and tomahawked on the spot. Thus fell the best negro I ever owned, and for whom I had often refused three hundred dollars.

When the Indians had plundered the canoe of my effects, they wantonly set fire to her, and burned her to the water's edge. The canoe had cost me ninety dollars, and was almost without an equal.

Having loaded three horses with plunder, the Indians dragged us to their flying-camp, about a mile in the woods, where we found several women and girls, stewing venison for supper in a loblolly-pot.

Perceiving the tenderness I felt towards my wife, they were under no fear that I should attempt to escape; but entertaining suspicions of negro Jack, they secured him during the night in a very effectual manner. They cut down a sapling the size of a man's thigh, and having made notches in it to receive the negro's legs, placed over each a pole, which they crossed with stakes driven on each side into the ground, and in the crotchets of the stakes they placed other poles, or rides. This confined the prisoner on his back; and, for their greater security, they put a thong of leather round his neck and fastened it to a tree.

I made a bed for Fanny and myself, by strewing branches on the ground; and obtained after much entreaty, a blanket for a covering. It may reasonably be expected that in this melancholy condition sleep was a stranger to our eyelids.

The next morning the Indians painted my wife red and black, and Jack with the same colour; but I was smutted over with black only. By this mark I knew they had devoted me to death; but I carefully concealed my suspicions from my wife.

With the rising sun we jogged forward towards the mountains. The company consisted of twelve Indian warriors, six squaws, three boys of twelve years, five children in arms; my wife and her child, myself, negro Jack, and Richard Edwards, the white man, who had decoyed us on shore. To this group must be superadded the three horses, loaded with the plunder of my boat.

It was a beautiful sun-rising. All nature seemed refreshed, and the dew fell drop by drop from the trees of the forest.

The wild turkeys were calling to each other from the lofty branches of the oak: the cardinal was expanding his golden plumage to the sun; the woodpecker was sticking his beak at the worms in the bark; and the mocking songster, with faint carol, was hailing the return of day.

We had not proceeded a mile, when an Indian picked up the scalp of a white man, which he presented to Namasket, the chief of the party.

I could perceive the roses fly the cheek of Fanny, on beholding this spectacle.

Proceeding onward, I eased my wife of the child, and carried it myself. When it was froward, the mother would take him and give him the breast.

One of the Indian women, who had no milk in her breast, wanted my wife to suckle her child. This I would not suffer. Upon which Squanto, the husband (the fellow who tomahawked Cuffey), was so incensed that he not only insulted Fanny, but filled the child's mouth with sand.

I could not contain myself: I snatched a tomahawk from the hand of an Indian who stood next to me, and called to Squanto to defend himself. He made a vigorous onset at me with his war-club. I evaded it by jumping on one side, and with the tomahawk I struck him a blow on the head which instantly deprived him of life.

On seeing Squanto fall, several of the Indians discovered great rage, and approached to dispatch me. A might strife ensued among them: some would kill me; others would prevent it: and thus one Indian was striving with another.

Fanny had clung to me, determined to share my fate. I loved her with all the feelings of a man; and it was not without secret satisfaction, that I reflected, the immortal part of us would both visit the other world together. I therefore suffered her to cling to me, and called to the Indians,—"*Tapoy! Tapoy! Pe quish a con gau mowon! manitowwhi gau no mun isse e to ta!*"—"Indians! Indians! Strike us all three, let us all die together!"

The hand of our destiny interposed to save us. Namasket was disposed in our favour; in which disposition he was confirmed by the cries of a beautiful Indian girl, whom he had but very lately married.

His voice restrained the arms and fury of the Indians. A kind of debate was held: a grave was dug, the dead Indian interred, and a quantity of stones piled over the spot.

Pocasset was the girl who had interceeded for us with the chief. She was the most beautiful Indian I ever saw—abounding in wild graces.

In the contention between the Indians, a circumstance happened, which when they were retored to their reason, not a little disquieted them. My negro, watching the concurrent of opportunity, had taken to his heels; and no sooner was he missed, than the eye of every Indian flamed with indignation.

It was Namasket who regulated their motions. He dispatched six of his fleetest Indians to seek for the negro, in different directions, and halted with the rest under the shade of a cypress. The cypress is the loftiest of the American trees: on its top the eagle builds her nest, and the crane finds a resting-place.

The squaws now kindled a fire, and put some Indian corn down to roast. Of this delicious food Pocasset tendered some to Fanny; and they ran to a spring to fill a gourd with water for her.

Nor were these all her good offices. She spoke to Namasket, and obtained from him permission to intermix some red spots with the black that covered my face and arms.

In an hour the Indians returned, but without having found negro Jack.

A profound gravity was now maintained among them for some minutes; when they jumped from the ground, on which they had formed a circle, and we prosecuted our journey.

I secretly rejoiced that negro Jack had escaped the vigilance of the

Indians. I could rely on the fellow's sense, fidelity and zeal; and a vision of deliverance took possession of my fancy.

Towards night-fall, the Indians took up their lodgings in a deserted wigwam, covered with bark. Namasket, and three others, then went out fire-hunting; which is worthy of being described.—

Having set fire to the woods, in a circular direction, the deer assembled instinctively in the middle, to avoid suffocation, puffing and blowing, and writhing their bodies. At length, oppressed with the encreasing volumes of smoke, they hung down their heads, stood motionless, and fell an easy prey to the hunters, who beating out their brains, dragged them from the flames.

The party revelled on venison, before they lay down to rest; and I was glad to see Fanny eat with a good appetite.

Canes were lighted, as an equivalent for candles: and an Indian boy was placed at the corner of the wigwam, to keep watch. Every half hour it was his duty to shout, and to give more horror to the sound, he put his finger between his lips. If the boy was remiss in making this clamour an Indian immediately rose and pummelled him with his fist till he roared with anguish.

At breakfast the following morning, Namasket found something that amused him for an hour. I had taught him to open a tea-chest, that was among our goods in the boat; and his supreme delight was to lock and unlock it, wondering how such a slight turn of his hand could have such an effect on the lid and the chest.

Europeans may laugh at the amusement of this Indian, but are they more rationally employed? Look at the people of London and Philadelphia! To me these cities present nothing but nurseries, filled with children of large growth! the girls are busy in dressing dolls, and the boys in playing at chuck-farthing, or driving a hoop. All are frivolously employed; every thing is vain, puerile, fantastic; and the world resembles the shew-box of the vagrant savoyard.

We prosecuted our journey through spreading forests of oak and hickory, from whose stately trees a long and shining moss depended, as far as the eye could see. The woods rang with a loud and melodious note of the red-bird; and every where the woodpecker was heard, though he could not be seen.

About noon we reached an Indian town, composed of a few huts; where we found the chief warrior on his death-bed.

Image to your mind, the hoary chief, weighed down with years, indulging the retrospect of the enemy that had fallen into his hands, and triumphing over the recollection of the groans produced by the infliction of slow torture! His only heaven is the country beyond the hills; its highest pleasure, food without the toils of the chase. The grounds of his hope are the trophies of his cruelty. He points to the scalps that hang round his wigwam. He charges the youthful warrior to emulate his deeds, and revenge him of his enemies.

In this day's march Richard Edwards, in beating for game, had lost his way in the woods. He overtook us at the village, fatigued beyond description; and the Indians were much delighted at the perplexing situation he had been in.

This Edwards was a miserable fellow. The Indian lasses having scorned his addresses, he had married an old squaw, whose decrepit form was disgusting in the highest degree. He was good for nothing but to chap wood, light fires, and fetch water.

The weather being very hot, and having no salt, our venison soon became putrid, and full of maggots. Yet the Indians and Edwards ate of it without reserve. I should have mentioned, that on approaching the village, our Indians begun their customary whooping, to announce they were coming with prisoners. They issued a dismal yell, to denote that one of their party was slain; and sent forth two warhoops, to proclaim they had brought home two captives.

On leaving the village, my wife's feet being sore with walking, Namasket mounted her upon one of the horses; and I now journeyed forward with a lighter heart.

We had hitherto kept towards the mountains; but the Indians being of opinion that they had sufficiently eluded pursuit, our party again bent their course towards the river Ohio.

On the evening of the third day, we fell in with a party of Indians, who were conducting a white planter and his negro slave, whom they had made captives, to their town.

It seems, the master, in the insolence of prosperity, had exercised the whip of power over the back of the negro. This tyranny the negro had imparted to the Indians. The Indians abhorring slavery, turned the tables on the white man. He told the slave to flog his master. Sambo did not want to be conjured nor exhorted. To work the fellow went; and when we encountered the party, the planter was roaring like a bull-calf under the stripes of his slave.

Bidding farewell to these Indians, we travelled very hard that day, passing through several swamps, and crossing many brooks. We took up our night's lodging near a river that fell into the Ohio, where, after a poor meal, the Indians would have my wife to sing them a song. The song she sung them, was a passage from the Psalms, which made her dearer to me than ever.—

"*By the rivers of Babylon, there we sat down! Yea, we wept, when we remembered Zion. We hanged our harps upon the willows in the midst thereof! For they that carried us away captive, required of us a song; and they that wasted us, required of us mirth!*"

The emotions raised in my bosom by Fanny's affecting song, soon gave place to others of a less tender nature. The Indian boys made a drum by covering a deep bowl with deer-skin, and began to beat it with a stick. Another boy accompanied this music with shaking a rattle made of a gourd, put on a stick with small stones in it. The men set up a hideous howling, and the women began to dance, continuing their pastime till midnight, when they fell asleep.

On approaching the Ohio, the caution of the Indians returned. In extinguishing their fires they covered the ashes with leaves, that the white people might not trace them.

We now fared worse, too, than we had hitherto done. The Indians were afraid to kill game, lest the noise of the guns should alarm the white traveller; and we fed chiefly on squirrels, hedge-hogs and possums.

We encamped the next night at the falls of a small river. The Indian method of encamping is, to light a large fire, around which the party lie upon the grass, wrapped up in blankets, with their feet towards it.

I recollect under every circumstance of time and place, the evening of our third day's journey. Not a cloud obscured the sun, disappearing among the forests of the West. A cooling air shook the foliage of the trees, and the shrill hissing of the locust echoed from the oak.

Fanny seemed to enjoy the scene. A smile of enchantment graced her cheek as she hung with maternal fondness over her babe: in her looks was placid resignation; and she seemed to hear the voice of God whispering consolation in the evening breeze.

Pursuing our journey, we came next to the Ohio.

The Indians encamped in a wood near the river's bank and held a consultation, of which I was the subject.

It was concerted that in the night, on the approach of a boat, I should run to the water, and practise the same arts used by Edwards, to decoy the passengers on shore; when, the Indians were to rush from their hiding-place, and massacre the whole, without distinction to colour, age, or sex.

This project appeared to me so abominable, that I told Namasket I would suffer death, rather than execute it. On hearing this, the

Indians laughed heartily, and told Edwards to get ready; promising him, in the event of a rich capture, to give him his liberty.

But the miserable jerry was, it seemed, under the dominion of the old squaw, his red wife; for he made answer that, having become an Indian by adoption, he abjured the white tribe, and preferred roving in the wilderness, to living in a town.

About ten at night, an Indian, who had been placed on the look-out, stole to our encampment, and acquainted his comrades that a boat with several men and women on board, was coming down the river.

On hearing this intelligence, the colour of poor Fanny went and came, and a convulsive shudder seized her form. I bade her be composed, and remember that the protecting arm of the Almighty Power was extended through universal space to defend the good from the wicked.

At length we could hear the noise of the rowers. The Indians nodded to Edwards, who crawled to the bank of the river, and set up the most dismal cries that human lips could utter.

The people in the boat lay upon their oars.

"Take me! oh! take me on board," cried he. "Save a poor wretch from famine, and God will reward you all. For five days have I wandered through woods, wet with the dews of heaven, and clinging to the rock for want of a shelter."

A debate now arose in the boat, whether they should take him on board or not. Some were for the motion, others against it.

Edwards redoubled his lamentations and entreaties.

He was answered from the boat, by a man in the New England dialect.

"I say, my friend!" cried the man, "if you ever come on board of this boat, you must swim off to her. But I vow, the boat shall not go to you. I guess you are an imposter. But be that as it may, I declare you will not easily trick Jonathan Oakes, who was educated at the college of Cambridge, in Massachusets, and who married a third cousin of Benjamin Franklin."

"I cannot swim," cried Edwards. "Nay I have not strength to move."

"I will soon see that," cried the yankee. And so saying, he discharged a musket loaded with small shot over the head of the kneeling supplicant.

Edwards on hearing the shot whiz by him, jumped from the ground, and ran precipitately from the riverside.

A hearty laugh ensued among the people on board the boat.

"Yes, yes!" cried Jonathan; "I guessed I could give you a dose of my pills, that would soon restore your strength."

The boat now proceeded down the river, amidst the hootings of the boatmen, who called out contemptuously, "*Uke Tapoy?*" "Where are the Indians?"

During this scene the Indians lay so still, that not a leaf was heard to rustle. But when the boat was out of hearing, they rose in great wrath, and began to upbraid Edwards for not having practised his arts and stratagems effectually.

Edwards endeavoured to exculpate himself; but they would not hear his defence. They rose upon him with great fury, and began to beat him with their fists. The fellow roared with pain; and I know not how far the wrath of the Indians would have carried them, had not the old squaw interposed, and pulled away her husband from their chastisement.

Fearful of a pursuit, the Indians immediately broke up their camp, and took the path towards the mountains, travelling over large creeks, swamps and rugged hills.

Fanny still rode the horse, and I walked by her side, carrying our child in my arms.

We had travelled about fifteen miles, when the Indians divided into two parties. Namasket continued his course with one division towards the interior; and the other Indians, five in number, again bent their way towards the Ohio, taking with them Edwards, my wife and her child, together with myself.

The names of the Indians of our party were, Sequassan, the chief; Matoona, his wife; Chillaback, Narraganset, and Arnmonoscoggin.

Sequassan had clad himself in a motley garb, half Indian and half English. He had on a waistcoat, breeches, shoes, and a hat; but for a coat he wore a deer-skin; and his long hair was tied up in a knot behind, somewhat in the fashion of a horse's tail.

It was with regret that Fanny separated from Pocasset, and I took a kind farewell of Namasket, who told me at parting, that he loved the whites, and would always befriend them.

Having taken a circuitous route, and being under no apprehension of alarm, the Indians again approached the Ohio.

They had not been encamped long, when a boat was heard at a distance. It was evening, the bat was wheeling his flight through the air, and the whip-poor-will was welcoming the approach of darkness.

The Indians kept close in a wood adjoining the river, and when the boat got abreast the spot, Edwards threw himself on his knees, and with uplifted hands accosted the rowers.

"Have pity!" cried he, "upon an unhappy forlorn wretch, who, for nine long days has been wandering in these woods, without any shelter but the canopy of heaven, and with scarce enough sustenance to support animal life. Oh! receive me, or I perish!"

The supplicant was now answered by a man in the boat. "My friend," said he, "your condition touches my heart. I will take you on board."

The boat approached the shore.

Edwards, as it had been preconcerted, whistled when she touched the ground. The Indians rushed from their hiding-place, and made a vigorous onset against the whites. But how much were they deceived. The white people, prepared for their coming, met the assault with such determined skill, firmness, and courage, that soon Sequassan fell, Chillaback gnawed the dust, Narraganset measured his length on the ground, and Arnmonoscoggin took to flight. While a boy of fourteen, boiling with rage, stepped up to Edwards, who was trying to escape, and knocked out his brains with one of the boat's stretchers.

At this moment the triumph of the boat's crew was somewhat damped by the war-hoop of several Indian voices in the woods. I instantly conveyed my wife and child into the boat, and clamoured for a musket. A musket was put into my hand by one of the party, and I got ready to oppose the enemy with the rest.

"Stranger," said the head of the party, "I love you for your courage, but let us not be indiscreet. The voices are numerous that come from the woods. We are only seven in number. Let us get into the boat, and gain the middle of the stream."

The advice was approved, and followed. We gained the middle of the river, and lay on our oars. Nor had we been there a minute, when at least fifty Indians came running towards the bank, brandishing their arms and uttering the war-hoop.

Fanny shrieked with affright. But we, levelling our pieces, gave them such a volley, that seven of them fell; and before we could repeat our fire, the rest ran back howling to the woods.

We now proceeded down the river, and I was landed by Mr Thatcher, my deliverer, at the place of my destination.

It seems my negro who had escaped from the party, had reached a town on the Ohio, and put the people on their guard against the tricks of the Indians. Mr Thatcher had heard of my captivity, and longed to be the instrument of my emancipation. Hence the vigour with which he received the assault of the Indians, and their total discomfiture.

Such was the narrative of Mr Keith, which fixed the attention of his audience, by shewing in strong colours how guilt was punished, and dismissing to happiness the pair for whom their passions and reason were equally interested.

Chapter 12

THE first inquiry made by captain Brilliant related to the naval force of the enemy, in that part of the world; and to his satisfaction, he learned, there was a frigate of superior force to his own lying at that time in Hampton Roads.

The same afternoon a pilot-boat passed the *Desdemona*, which the captain hailed.

"Do you know that frigate in Hampton Roads?"

"Yes! I carried her in. She is the finest ship that ever yet fought her guns upon one deck. She has fourteen ports of a side, and carries eighteen-pounders. A warm ship. She shews her teeth bravely!"

"Huzza! beauty!" cried captain Brilliant: "There will be some honour for us to engage her. My little *Desdemona* has only thirteen ports of a side, and only carries twelves; yet I am of opinion we could hammer the dust out of her."

"My dear Brilliant," said Cassandra, "I trust you only jest. Your country expects from you courage, but not rashness."

"Make yourself easy, Cassandra," returned the captain; "with the ship's company I command, there would be no rashness in bringing the largest French frigate to action that ever swam salt water."

Cassandra sighed mournfully.

"Mrs Hurricane," resumed Brilliant, "do you not wish to be the wife of a master and commander?"

"I am very content with my present husband, sir," replied Flora.

"Yes," rejoined the captain; "but if we take this frigate, your husband will be promoted."

The next day captain Brilliant worked his ship into Hampton Roads, where he found the republican frigate lying at anchor, all a-taunt-o, that is, ready for sea. He brought up his ship in grand style, furling sails with an expedition scarcely to be conceived, and squaring his yards with the nicest precision.

The pilot had not made use of any hyperbolical amplification, when he described the French frigate. She was, indeed, the finest ship that ever fought her guns upon one deck.

Be ever memorable the morning of January the first, 1801, which heaped fresh honours on the sons of Britannia! Oh! fleeting Time! scatter, if thou wilt, the rest of these pages to the winds of heaven; but let that be sacred which records the achievements of Neptune's legitimate children!

At eight o'clock both ships crossed their topgallant yards; and in somewhat more than half an hour, the boatswain on board the French frigate piped the hands aloft to weigh anchor, and her fore-topsail was loosened, as a signal for sailing.

Captain Brilliant lost no time to do the same. His fore-topsail was in a moment cast loose from the yard; the capstern bars were manned, the cat-fall overhauled down; and as a kind of challenge, the tompions were taken out of the main-deck guns.

The French frigate had now weighed, and stood out of the bay, with her jack, ensign, and pendant flying; nor did an interval of a minute elapse before the anchor of the *Desdemona* was hove up to the bow, and sail made on the ship.

No sooner had both ships gained an offing than the French frigate hauled up her foresail, took in her topgallant-sails, and hove to for the *Desdemona*, whose inferiority of sailing was manifest, and who was crowding every stitch of canvas to come within gunshot of her opponent. Upon which captain Brilliant took in his royals, and his ship's company manning the shrouds, gave three hearty cheers.

But before we enter the scene of combat, let us contemplate one of a more tender nature.

I behold Cassandra descending to the cockpit, supported by her husband, her eyes streaming in tears, and her hair dishevelled. I behold jealousy giving way to love in the bosom of Flora, and anger surpassed by solicitude for her lieutenant. But neither the mournful distraction of Cassandra, nor the apprehensions of Flora, can withhold their lovers from the quarter-deck of battle.

The men, fore and aft, were now at their quarters, and captain Brilliant, looking over the break of the quarter-deck, vociferated to them through his speaking-trumpet,

"Stand by, my boys!"

"All ready!" was the reply.

Upon which our hero ran up alongside the French frigate; and, calling to his people, "Fire away!" they discharged their broadside, which was returned by the enemy before the sound was out of the *Desdemona's* guns.

The action thus begun, was continued on board the *Desdemona* with that cool intrepidity which is the distinguishing characteristic of British seamen; and captain Brilliant discovered that he was both a sailor and an officer, for he both worked and fought his own ship.

And on the quarter-deck of glory were to be seen, the master anticipating the orders of the captain; the marine officer firing his division over the quarter; and lieutenant Hurricane calling to the men at the quarter-deck guns and carronades, "Keep yourselves cool, my lads! Mind the heave of the sea! Now, strike it into her!"

The two ships had now got close to each other, exchanging their compliments yard-arm and yard-arm; a practice introduced by Benbow, and revived by Anson.

At this period, the hammocks in the quarter-deck nettings of the *Desdemona* caught fire, from a wad of the enemy; upon which young Echo, of whom we have before spoken, jumped upon his gun, and lugging out his knife, cut them away overboard.

"Bravo! Echo!" exclaimed captain Brilliant—but before he could utter more, an eighteen pound shot tore up the bulwark, and made the splinters fly in every direction; laying flat on the deck, some on their backs and some on their faces, the following officers and men:

Robert Soundings, master.

Francis Easy, the marine officer.

Thomas Wilson, quarter-master.

John Pearce, captain of the after-guard.

Hugh Vincent, ordinary seaman; and

Mars Mattocks, a marine.

"Jump here! bear a hand!" vociferated lieutenant Hurricane, "and carry Mr Soundings into the cockpit. A blasted shot that! Messmate, are you much wounded?"

"I fear," faultered the master, "my grog is stopped."

"And how are you, my dear Easy?" said Hurricane.

"I feel," replied the marine officer, "I shall have to capitulate! Death has already put his storming ladder to my soul! I die! I die! My God! My God!"

"Are you much hurt, Pearce?" inquired Hurricane.

"Yes, sir," replied the captain of the after-guard, "that shot cut away my lifelines! My soul is unreeving! O Peggy! Peggy! My wife! My dear wife!"

About this period the colours of the enemy disappeared.

"She has struck!" cried an Irish landsman in the waist.

"Struck!" retorted captain Brilliant. "By heaven! you may strike first yet. Does she slacken fine? Is it the guns or the colours you judge by?"

The captain had scarce finished speaking, when a new pair of colours were hoisted by the enemy. Her ensign had been shot away.

A sailor from each of the quarter-deck guns had now left his station, to carry the wounded down into the cockpit; and a couple of stout lads had got hold of the master, whom they were lugging to the hatchway.

"Avast there!" cried captain Brilliant, "with the master. He has struck! The soul of as good a seaman as ever took hold of the helm of a vessel, is gone aloft to heaven!"

"Jump to the marine officer!" cried lieutenant Hurricane.

"By——!" said captain Brilliant, "it is of no use. The marine officer has resigned his commission. Look to Pearce, the captain of the after-guard. How is it with him?"

"He is gone, sir," replied lieutenant Hurricane, "upon the same tack as the marine officer. He has answered the muster of death."

At this juncture a crash was heard in the main-deck, which was followed by doleful groans.

"Jump, Mr Echo," said the captain, "into the waist: the frenchman's shot is playing at hell and turn-up-jack there!"

The midshipman soon returned.

"A shot, sir," said Mr Echo, "has dismounted one of the midship guns, killed the third lieutenant, and wounded almost every man at the gun."

"What!" cried lieutenant Hurricane, "has death dropped the peak of my messmate, poor Balcony!"

"Huzza! my sons!" cried captain Brilliant to the people at the main-deck guns. "Beauty! that's the fire!"—

The exhortations of captain Brilliant were interrupted by the carpenter. He came upon deck to acquaint the captain that the enemy's shot had taken such effect, that there were several feet water in the well; and that even if recourse were had to the pumps, it would be impracticable to keep the ship half an hour above water.

"Be it so! Mr Chips," said the captain. "But hark you! say not a word about the matter. I will soon have a clear well."

The two frigates were now so close along-side of one another, that their yard-arms were mutually locked by their rigging.

"Hurricane!" cried captain Brilliant, "I will board the Frenchman in the smoke. Hark you, call the boarders. I will put myself at their head. In the mean time, be ready yourself to follow me with a fresh gang of volunteers."

The boarders now assembled, to the amount of seventy; men equal to any heroic enterprize; men who would have gone through flames, had their duty imposed on them the task. They were armed with cutlasses and pistols.

"Are you ready? my sons!" cried captain Brilliant.

"All ready, sir!" was the reply.

"Then follow me!" cried the hero.

Captain Brilliant now boarded the enemy's ship, followed by his men, who were all contending for the honour of fighting by his side.

The French officers and sailors collected to oppose the assailants. But such was the discipline, such the intrepidity of the British tars, that resistance was of no avail. Brilliant with his troop of boarders, made their way through a host of enemies. The first lieutenant followed in succession with volunteers from the ship's company; and the *Desdemona,* like the fabled horse of Troy, poured out heroes from her womb!

The Frenchmen called for quarter. But before they had made the supplication, young Echo had got aft and hauled down their colours.

The sailors now filled the air with acclamations of triumph; the surviving officers shook hands with each other; and no time was lost in securing the prisoners.

"Hurricane," said captain Brilliant, "step on board the *Desdemona*, and see how the women come on. I begin now to think of my wife."

"Aye aye! sir!" cried the lieutenant.

Let us now turn our eyes from the quarter-deck of battle, to a scene of a softer nature. Let us contemplate Flora, leaning on the shoulder of her cherishing lieutenant; and Cassandra with eager eye and panting bosom, seeking for her lord. Behold these tender and faithful spirits meet. Behold Cassandra stepping over the mangled bodies of the slain! Behold her flying to the warm embrace of her husband!

"My dear! dear Brilliant!" faultered Cassandra.

Brilliant made no reply: but his heart glowed within him, as he pressed his fair bride to his breast, who fainted in his arms.

And now the cry was, that the *Desdemona* was going down. She was, in fact, literally sinking; and the French frigate had not been disentangled fifteen minutes from her, before she went down.

Mr Taffarel, young Echo, and about a dozen other excellent swimmers, kept on board the *Desdemona* to the last, busied in cutting loose her boats, and the spars they were stowed on. By which means the barge, and several spare topmasts were saved.

And presently was to be seen this adventurous gang jumping from the *Desdemona* into the sea, and cleaving the waves with the lusty strokes of their arms, to escape being swallowed up in the vortex of the sinking wreck.

Chapter 13

THE name of the captured frigate was *le Fripon*, mounting forty-two guns, and carrying four hundred and fifty men. Captain Brilliant having consigned the bodies of his slaughtered foes to the bosom of the ocean, made sail upon her, and shaped his course again for Hampton Roads, where he repaired the damages she had sustained.

The prisoners were now landed; and Mr Echo, who had so conspicuously distinguished himself on the deck of glory, was made lieutenant in the place of the one who had been slain. Thus the shot that levels one man elevates another.

Captain Brilliant continued to cruize three months off the capes of Virginia, when he again sailed for England, having his brows entwined both with heroic and domestic laurels; for he had not only triumphed in battle with the foe, but made an achievement of a more delicious warfare. I will not romantically assert, that Cassandra was growing more lovely to the sight, but she was every day getting bigger: and that shape, which was once distinguished for its being small by degrees and beautifully less, had now no pretensions to spiral tenuity.

Nor was Mrs Hurricane without an accession to her size. In fact, she had swollen to such a magnitude, that, to appropriate the words of her husband, she measured in circumference more than the main-mast;

"Bravo!" Brilliant would say

The captain's lady
Is always ready
  To go a cruise!

"Do I not, my dear Brilliant," said Cassandra, "make a very good sailor?"

"Yes; but you must not keep abaft."

"Why so?"

"Why, because you will bring the ship down by the stern."

In this manner would the captain rally his fair spouse, who was now sufficiently mistress of the vocabulary of a ship to know what he would be at.

Indeed, the novels which both Cassandra and Flora had brought on board, were neglected for Falconer's *Marine Dictionary*, which, from being sailors' wives, they studied with enthusiasm.

It was the time of the full-moon, when our noble sea-officers approached their native land, and towards night. Many of the sailors affirmed, that they could smell the coal fires of John English.

But this was a mistake; for captain Brilliant by keeping in an easterly direction, hugged the French coast, in the hope that he should also hug a few French merchantmen.

It was ten at night. The full moon was reflected from the deep, and the ship with graceful motion was breasting the lofty surge! Lieutenant Echo had the watch; and the helmsman responded to the cry of the quarter-master who, looking at his compass, called, "Steady along! Steady!"

Mr Hurricane and his wife, if I may so express myself, had turned in; but captain Brilliant was leaning with Cassandra over the quarter, enjoying the solemn beauty of the scene before them.

Lieutenant Echo (I love to call him by his new title) was walking the deck, in company with Mr Gale, one of his late messmates. Lieutenant Echo had derived some consequence from the accession of his lappels; and though not confirmed, he looked upon himself as a lieutenant, which was just the same thing. But his former companions would not acknowledge his title in private. They called him Acting Dickey; in fact, they asserted he was only half a luff-tackle.

"Is that young gentleman," said Cassandra, pointing to Mr Echo, "the person who fought so gallantly in the action?"

"He is, my dear," replied Brilliant.

"Has he a mother or a sister, my love?"

"No, my dear."

"Oh! if he had, how their hearts would be rejoiced."

Let me be pardoned for making the captain and his lady couple love and dear in their colloquy of the night. More real conjugal affection will be found within the confines of a ship, than the precincts of a house. A ship has never any fashionable couple who require separate beds; but Jack and his wife are always content to swing together in one hammock.

"A sail, hoa!" vociferated a fellow on the forecastle.

Lieutenant Echo danced forward.

"Three sail right a-head!" exclaimed the young lieutenant.

"Steady so, then!" cried captain Brilliant. "Get a gun ready forward there."

"Aye, aye! sir!" replied Mr Echo, seizing a handspike to point one of the bow guns, which the captain of the forecastle cast loose. Young

Gale jumped below for a match.

"All ready with the gun, sir!" vociferated Mr Echo.

"Good God!" cried Cassandra. "In pity what is all this? Oh, do not fire!"

"Keep all fast there!" said the captain. "My wife will miss stays."

The captain had now got his night-glass upon deck, and was surveying the three vessels. They were evidently merchantmen. It was time to shorten sail; the frigate was coming up with the strange ships hand over hand. The top-gallant sails were therefore clued up, and people stood ready to back the main topsail.

In a few minutes the *Fripon* got into the midst of the vessels.

"Hoa! The ship a-hoy! Hoa! hoa!" etc.

They were three large ships deeply laden, from Saint Domingo. Joyful was the news. The boatswain's mate piped the ship's company up.

"All hands to take possession of the prizes ahoy!"

Lieutenant Hurricane left the arms of his wife, and ran upon deck half dressed.

"See what luck I always bring in my watch," said Echo.

"So I think I heard you say," returned Hurricane.

"Shall we toss out the boats, sir?" said Mr Hurricane.

"Certainly," replied the captain.

"Up there, topmen!" cried Mr Hurricane, "and clap on the yard tackles. Get the stays to pass there! Where is the after-guard? Stretch along your tacke-fall here!"

And now came Flora upon the deck; her long dark hair floating luxuriantly down her back, and waving its ringlets to the breeze of the night.

"My dear Hurricane," said she, "what made you leave me? I am sure you have every convenience in your cabin, without being obliged to go upon deck."

"My dear," said the lientenant, "we have taken three French merchantmen. Our fortune is made. You will have to go prize-master of one of them. Get up, therefore, you chart of the Channel, and stand by to go in the boat."

"Indeed though I shan't. I won't leave you."

The boats were now tossed out; the prizes were taken possession of; and onwards they jogged, accompanied by *le Fripon*, who, with her topsails on the cap, went three feet to their one.

The ships having altered their course, it was judged prudent at daylight to try for soundings. The frigate was hove to.

"The line," said a lieutenant, "is passed along!"

"All ready with the lead!"

"Heave away!" cried Mr Hurricane.

"Watch there!" "Watch!" vociferated the seamen in succession.

They got ground with ninety fathoms. The vessels filled. The Start Point was made at an early hour in the morning, and the wind blowing strong from the westward, they were wafted with rapidity up Channel.

"We go extremely fast," said Cassandra. "Is not the wind very fair?"

"It is too fair, my dear," replied the captain. "I know not on which side to carry my spankerboom."

The *Fripon* sailed into Spithead with the British colours flying over French, and was cheered by the men-of-war that were lying at anchor.

The letter of captain Brilliant, which described his action, had been received at the Admiralty by the Norfolk Packet. It was short. True valour delights more in action than words.

Sir,

I have the honour to acquaint you, that on January 1, 1801, *I worked his Majesty's ship the* Desdemona, *out of Chesapeak Bay, in company with the republican French frigate* le Fripon*; and having gained a sufficient offing to come to battle, we commenced close action; when the superior metal of the enemy caused the* Desdemona *to make so much water, that the carpenter informed me the ship was going down. Upon hearing this, I called my boarders, and carried the enemy in the smoke. Every officer, seaman and marine did their duty.*

I regret the loss of Sam. Soundings, master; Thomas Balcony, third lieutenant, and Evelyne Easy, officer of marines; together with seven seamen killed.

I am, etc.
BRYAN BRILLIANT.

And now the heart of Cassandra beat with tenfold joy, first, that she was restored to her native land; and secondly, because a peace was impending between England and France.

The report was true. The *Fripon* had not been five days at Spithead, when peace was proclaimed, and her officers and men paid off.

Chapter 14

MRS BRILLIANT now thought of the admiral, her uncle; but here she was anticipated; for before she had composed a letter, she received one from that worthy man, replete with tender congratulations and enclosing another not less cordial to her intrepid husband.

They were both earnestly invited to pass the peace in Wales, which they readily accepted; stipulating, however, to reside one month in the vicinity, where our noble captain had some official business to transact.

He hired a convenient house at Chelsea, where he took up his abode with his beloved spouse, together with Mr and Mrs Hurricane, and lieutenant Echo to whom he was attached from the noblest sentiment.

"Here are excellent apartments, Hurricane," said he. "Here we may sleep with our wives, and be under no fear of bringing our anchors home."

"Right, sir," replied Hurricane.

"And I say," resumed the captain, "if it is a son that you have laid down the keel of, what will you call him?"

"I will name him after you, sir. I will call him Bryan Brilliant Hurricane."

"Bravo!" said the captain. "But our wives are both thieves."

"Thieves!" exclaimed the ladies.

"Yes," rejoined the captain. "You are come on shore with half a dozen pursers' bread-bags under your aprons."

"My wife," said Hurricane, "looms like Beachy Head."

"And my wife," answered the captain, "looms like Beachy Head in a fog."

And here they both laughed heartily in concert.

In a short time more, the *Fripon's* prize money was paid. It amounted to a large sum. It was sufficient to enable our three heroes to pass the rest of their lives in affluence; and as it was earned in the defence of their king and country, I am persuaded that none of my readers will envy them their wealth.

Captain Brilliant left Mr Hurricane to protect the ladies; and, accompanied by young Echo, proceeded to town, to the house of his agent, calling first at the Admiralty.

When captain Brilliant had transacted his official business, he called on Mr Million the banker, with an order for some money. I cannot be exact with regard to the sum.

Mr Million received our hero with particular attention, and expressed his wish to have the honour of the gallant captain's and the lieutenant's company that day at dinner. Brilliant accepted the invitation; and at four o'clock was put down, with Mr Echo, from a coach, at the door of the banker's house.

Captain Brilliant was shewn into the drawing-room, where he found Mr and Mrs Million, the two Miss Millions, and a young lady their cousin, assembled to receive him; together with Sir Jacob Stockfish, the Rev. Mr Cringewell, and the Earl of Bolton.

Of the young ladies, all were comely; but Miss Spa bore the bell. Her fine flaxen hair was elegantly turned above her head, and the ribbon which bound her tresses, was lost in their profusion. Her eyes were of a languishing blue; her lips full and ripe; her neck boded every symmetry, and her waist was gracefully slender. There was a dash of melancholy in her countenance, which became it more than smiles. It denoted a vacancy of heart, the want of some one object, some transported lover, on whom to fix her affections.

"You have never seen my son Caesar?" said Mr Million, addressing the captain.

"I never had that honour, sir."

"He is a fine youth. He was educated at Harrow, and did once know greek and latin. But he is now, ha! ha! ha! quite the military man. He is ensign of a volunteer corps. It would do you good to see him go through his manual and platoon exercise."

Captain Brilliant bowed.

"Between you and me and the post, he has recruited lately to some purpose; he has enlisted the heart (whispering) of Miss Spa, the young lady who sits next to my eldest daughter. It was his red coat did this. Women, like mackerel, (raising his voice) ha! ha! ha! are caught with a red bait."

"True, sir," said captain Brilliant. "The blue jackets stand no chance."

Sophonisba (Miss Spa) reddened. It was a blush of inconstancy. Before, the red coat of Caesar (which had transformed him from a Thersites into an Achilles) made Sophonisba's little heart flutter when he approached her; but from the moment the young lieutenant entered the room, all her love for the volunteer vanished, as though it had been by the stroke of an enchanter's wand.

In a few minutes more a servant announced at the door that ensign Caesar was returned from being reviewed by Sir Tottenham Turnstile, which gave immediate rise to the tenderest exclamations.

Mrs Million. Mary! Mary! make haste with the calf's foot jelly! Caesar is come.

Mary. Mamma, it is not ready yet.

Mrs Million. Not ready! Alas! Alas! My poor boy will be laid up again! He must be exhausted with marching! Tell John to run over to Pattypan's and get a fresh custard! My poor Caesar! I know his state! His ambition always makes him over-march himself.

And now entered ensign Caesar, accompanied by captain Shank. Two such men of war! They held themselves perfectly upright, neither inclining to the right nor left, the shoulders square and kept back, the breast advanced, the flat of the hands touching the thighs, the toes turned out; and they marched to ordinary time, keeping themselves dressed in a line, and both scrupulously observing the same length of pace.

At length captain Shank vociferated, "Halt!" when these warriors stopped and bowed to the company.

Captain Shank approached Miss Million, and Caesar threw himself into a chair, crossing his arms, and affecting to sleep.

Mrs Million. My dear boy, you have over-marched yourself. The jelly is not ready, but I have dispatched John for a custard.

Caesar (his eyes shut)—"Rear rank take close order! March! Make ready! Present! Fire!"

"Caesar," said Mrs Million, "you will frighten the ladies with your war-hoop. Sophonisba trembles like a leaf."

"Psha!" cried Caesar. "Sophonisba would soon let off a gun! Make ready! Present! Fire! Shank! was not our review noble?"

"Sublime! oh! sublime!" cried captain Shank. "But I am hoarse with giving the word of command. Battalion wheel back into open column! The right in front! Counter-march by files! Right face!—March! Officers dress your companies! Mr Million! Eyes right! Look less at the girls and more at your men."

"You be d—d!" cried Caesar. "Go to drill! Go to drill! Don't you quiz an old soldier."

"Old soldier!" cried captain Shank. "Why! powder and ball! I am twelve years older than you, and I have carried arms from my infancy. My ears have ever been familiar with the rattling drum, and the piercing fife. When a child, I panted for the musket; and when an apprentice, after shop-shutting, I learned the manual exercise of our porter, who had been a corporal in the militia. Caesar! traduce me not. Calumniate me not. Spare, spare your insinuation."

The footman now came to announce that dinner was on the

table: each gentleman seized a lady. Captain Shank gave his hand to the eldest Miss Million: the Earl of Bolton tended his to the sister, and captain Brilliant took the hand of Sophonisba—her military gallant withholding his escort.

When the company were seated, Caesar entered the room, and seemed disposed to take his seat at the end of the table; but his mother, worthy woman! thought carving would fatigue, and made him sit next to her, that he might enjoy the benefit of the fire. Caesar had marched from the Exchange to Hyde Park, and back again that day.

The dinner passed away after the usual routine. Each brought a good appetite; and Mr Million and Sir Jacob rolled their white eyes, and shook the green fat of their dew lapped visages, as they guttled down the callipash and callipee of a turtle.

All ate heartily but one, and that was Sophonisba.

"Sophonisba! child," exclaimed Mrs Million, "you eat like a sparrow! Don't grieve yourself about Caesar! He is pale only from over-marching himself. Let me give you this wing."

"Indeed, madam," said Sophonisba, "I have no appetite whatever."

"Ha!" cried Mr Million, with a profound look. "I remember that about this time thirty years—it was in my courtship—my wife could not eat. She lived entirely on love. Caesar! thou art a type of thy father; thou canst make an impression!"

Here the old man laughed heartily at his own penetration. Laughing is contagious.—"Ha! ha!" laughed the Earl; "Ha! ha!" reiterated the knight; "Ha! ha!" roared captain Shank.

And had the god of love inspired Sophonisba with a passion for Caesar? The God of heaven forbid! No! it was the person, the speech, the manners of the young naval hero, that deprived the nymph of her appetite; it was lieutenant Echo who had lighted up a flame in her breast, that the ocean could not extinguish.

Lieutenant Echo sat at table between Mrs Million and Sophonisba.

"Were you in the action, sir," said the good lady, "with captain Brilliant?"

"Yes, madam."

"And I dare affirm," said Mr Million, "the young man did honour to the wooden walls?"

"He did," observed captain Brilliant. "He saved the ship from catching fire, by cutting the hammocks overboard on the quarter-deck. He was among the foremost in boarding the enemy's frigate: he fought full an hour while smarting under his wounds; and it was not till he had hauled down the French colours with his own hands, that he thought of a surgeon."

"Noble!" said captain Shank. "My heart kindles at the recital! Oh! that I had been there!"

"It would have been hotter work," said Mr Million, "than firing with blank cartridges." And he laughed heartily.

There is something so noble in courage, that no breast can refuse it homage; but it takes particularly with the softer sex, who look to man for protection. While captain Brilliant was pronouncing the panegyric of Mr Echo, poor Sophonisba was over-come with emotion; her colour went and came; and she sighed pitiably, accompanying her sighs, with side glances at the young naval hero.

At length the ladies withdrew, when the men sat round their coal fire, and indulged over their bottle; where I shall leave them, to follow the lovely fair ones.

Chapter 15

SOPHONISBA took the first opportunity to steal to her chamber, where she could indulge undisturbed, the emotions raised in her bosom by the young naval hero. Her senses were bewildered; she leaned her glowing cheek upon her hand, and fetched a world of sighs. A miniature picture of Caesar, dressed in a flaming red coat, lay on her toilet; but she beheld it with scorn, crying, "Faugh!" as she looked towards it.

The god of darts, or love, or whatever the reader pleases to call the tenderest of all passions embodied, was now fanning the flame he had lighted up in the bosom of Sophonisba. Her imagination became every moment more heated. And partly by meditating on the agreeable qualities that really belonged to the young lieutenant, and partly by fancying others, her mind was become so attached to him, that it could not be separated from the cherished object, without pain or reluctance.

Captain Brilliant and lieutenant Echo were the first who retired from the parlour to the drawing-room, the citizens chusing to protract their drinking-bout.

The ladies had not yet descended from their respective chambers, the captain could, therefore, commune unheard with his young lieutenant.

"Hark you, Echo! If you don't make your fortune in less than a week, 'tis your own fault. You are a likely young fellow and if Sopha—Sophonisba (her name is as long as the fore-top-bowline) is not in love with you, there are no snakes in Virginia."

"Say you so, sir?"

"It is the case by all that's true! She could not keep her eyes off you at dinner. She looked cupids at you! I could see her heart move up and down like a brig's boom in a calm; and when I told the tough story about your courage, the poor girl changed colour in the face like a dolphin."

"She's a pretty creature, sir! I know she has given me the heart-ache! Such top-lights! such catheads! such a clean run from stem to stern! I could fight the devil to get spliced to her! I would battle the watch with fifty of her lobster lovers."

"Hark you! We are all going to the play. You range up along-side of her, and talk to her like a sailor-man."

"I am a bad hand at fine speeches along-side of a modest girl. Amongst the blowings in the Hay-market or about Covent-garden, I have more impudence than a highwayman; but a modest girl always heaves me aback, and I make stern-way."

"Damnation! I thought you had read lord Chesterfield! I am sure you had it in your birth."

"No, sir; it belonged to the boatswain."

"Well, no matter. You lose no opportunity to board Sophonisba. Board her with sugar-plum phrases. Call her your angel!—your darling—your box of diamonds!—Swear you adore her!—swear by your commission—swear by the god of war!"

"I will sir; I will."

"And squeeze her hand. But squeeze it gently—for your hand is hard—it may make her sing out."

"My hand, sir, is as hard as a three-inch plank!"

"No matter! It is the hand of a man! the hand of a sailor! Women love hard hands! They love a fist that can give a knock-down blow in their defence. And it is not expected from a sailor to have worn chicken-skin gloves. Fear nothing! Stetch out! Huzza! with the bow!"

At this juncture, Sophonisba entered the room, on light fantastic toe; but she seemed somewhat confused at meeting the captain and his young lieutenant.

Brilliant rose, and seizing the hand of Sophonisba, led her to a chair near the fire. He then seated himself next her.

"Good God!" cried he, "how lovely you look! I thought my wife handsome; but you! you are a goddess! Oh! that I were single! Caesar should die!"

"Dear me! captain, I hope you would not kill poor Caesar?"

"Poor Caesar! (eyeing her archly) a very proper epithet. But, seriously, (whispering) do you care for him a stiver?"

"Indeed, captain, I do."

"You do! I say, Sophonisba, you may tell that to the marines—but, God forgive my swearing—may I be d—d, if the sailors will believe it."

"Oh! fie! captain!"

"But this backing and filling is nonsense, I say, my angel! be not captivated with the colour of a coat but the merit of him who wears it. Now there stands a youth before you! a blue jacket; who is neither wanting in merit or accomplishments. He will fight like a Trojan, and can work a ship like a sailor. He did not crawl on board through the cabin-windows; he came in at the bows. Let me woo for him. I am his friend"—

"I have somewhere read, captain, that

> Friendship is constant in all other things,
> Save in the office and affairs of love;
> Therefore, all hearts, in love use your own tongues!"

"Bravo!—Echo! Speak up! Huzza! in the bow!"

"Madam.—Miss.—By my commission—by the god of love—the god of war—the God of heaven:—your presence has given me the heart-ache—and if that is not a symptom of true love, I don't know in what point of the compass it lies!"

"Indeed, sir, I am much flattered."

"No! Miss; I know not how to flatter. I am not a soldier; I am a rough-knot.—My box of diamonds! shall you go to-night to the play?"

"I fear not, sir. I must stay at home out of compliment to my cousin. Caesar, you know has over-marched himself."

"Then I will challenge Caesar! By the merciful God! I will compel him to use his sword in earnest! For I do love nothing in the world so well as you!"

"Bravo! my lieutenant! Huzza! in the bow! Sophonisba, in pity calm his transports. Tell him your love is reciprocal."

"Oh! let me hide my face! It is."

"There's for you! Did you hear that, Echo? The sweet maid says it is reciprocal."

"Reciprocal!"

"Yes, reciprocal! Sophonisba, my lieutenant is not sentimental. He knows no such rope in the ship. Protest you love him in your heart."

"Oh! spare my blushes."

"Protest it, or he'll go mad. His Majesty's service will lose a gallant young officer."

"Well, then, I so love him with my heart, that none is left to protest."

"What say you, Echo?"

"Oh! seas and skies! I am so happy! I am made post! I am more! I feel myself an admiral!"

"Hush!" cried Sophonisba; "I hear the company on the stairs. Change! change the subject!"

"Indeed, madam," said Brilliant; "I am heartily of your opinion. They make a most soldierly appearance: they would do honour to a veteran corps. I could scarce wish finer men to serve with."

During this eulogium, the gentlemen entered the room, flushed with drinking respectively a bottle.

"Rear rank, there! take close order!" cried captain Shank. "Advance in line! File and charge in to the front. Form open column of companies!"

Coffee succeeded; and during the regale, the naval gentlemen were invited to accompany the ladies to the theatre; but Caesar still continuing *unwell,* Sophonisba could not, from delicacy, make one of the party; and Brilliant, apprized of it, declined the invitation, and took leave of the family with his young lieutenant.

"Let this day," cried captain Brilliant, as he walked towards Temple-bar, arm-in-arm with his lieutenant: "let the events of this day, Echo, be recorded in the log-book of your life."

"Bestow your charity, my noble sea-officers," cried a one-legged sailor to our heroes.—"Bestow your charity upon poor Jack, who is hove to under a storm-stay-sail!"

"Here, shipmate!" cried Brilliant, "is half a crown for you."

"Here I come, sir," cried Jack, redoubling his agility—"here I crowd all the sail I have left!"

"And there's another half crown," said Echo.—"Luff, boy, luff! and catch it in your hat."

"God Almighty bless you both!" cried Jack. "I could tell you were seamen by the peak of your mizens. I might have begged of the red-jackets till all was blue again! Huzza! huzza! huzza!"

As our heroes passed along the Strand, they were accosted by a hundred gay ladies, who asked them if they were good natured.

"Devil take me!" exclaimed Echo, "if I know which way my ship heads: but there is not a girl in the Strand that I would touch with my gloves on."

"That will do for the marines," said captain Brilliant.

"Last night, sir, at this hour, I would have steered into the midst of the grand fleet. I would in a very short time have brought some ship to action; but now I luff up, I bear away to keep clear of them."

"You are in love, Echo, Hoa! the Sophonisba ahoy!"

"I will send to-morrow for a tailor: I will bend a new suit of sails."

"In love, by all that's true!"

"I will *fumigate* my pocket-handkerchief with lavender and *bergamyhot.*"

"In love, or I am not here!"

"I will improve myself in flute-playing."

"In love, to a certainty!"

"I will have my hanger new-mounted."

"In love, there's no doubt!"

"I will have my teeth cleaned by a dentist."

"In love, as sure as the devil's in London!"

At Piccadilly these heroes took a coach and proceeded to Chelsea; captain Brilliant sleeping the whole way, and Echo singing, as he looked towards the moon,

> "I saw her faint, or else 'twas fancy!"

Chapter 16

AT breakfast the next morning, the party were exceedingly merry at the recital given by captain Brilliant, and the confessions that the young lieutenant gave of his own heart.

"Why, this," cried Hurricane, "will be as good for you as a Spanish war. Twenty thousand pounds! It beats Flora's *sack* of half joes."

"Indeed, Hurricane," said Flora, "I wish it had been more. But I hope you are content."

"Is the lady beautiful?" said Hurricane.

"Faith! she is," returned the captain!—"Echo need never be in want of promotion while he has such a wife."

"Fie! captain," said Flora.

In a few days, Echo, who was impatient to obtain some tidings of Sophonisba, proposed that Hurricane should accompany him to town; and, taking a boat at the stairs, they were rowed down the river. But they had not proceeded far, when they descried another boat before them, filled with ladies and gentlemen, whose head was turning in every direction, the sail flapping against the mast, and the females screaming with mournful distraction.

"By the heavenly God!" exclaimed Echo, "I hear the voice of Sophonisba! Waterman! clap me alongside of that boat! Pull away! and be d—d to you!"

The breeze was freshening, the cries redoubled, and a youth who held the helm, was bawling for help! He was dressed in a red coat.

"A marine adrift upon a grating!" exclaimed Hurricane. "Oh, the Tom Bowers of a fellow! The wind right aft, and his boat yawing about like a dog in a fair! I'll be d—d, too, if his painter is not on fire!"

"Avast there!" cried Echo to the waterman: "way enough!" And he jumped from the wherry into the large boat, followed by Mr Hurricane.

Mr Echo grasped the tiller, Mr Hurricane trimmed the sail, and, in a moment, the boat stemmed majestically the stream.

"Harry!" cried Echo to his brother lieutenant, "do steer the boat, while I support that lady." And flying to Sophonisba, he took her in his arms.

"All is well, my box of diamonds!" whispered Echo.

"Oh! I'm so terrified!"

"Be not scared; you are safe with me."

"Am I?"

"Yes, indeed!" And so saying, he unobserved by all but Hurricane, glued his lips to those of Sophonisba, who suffered him to riot in the intoxicating draught of pleasure.

"Bravo!" cried Hurricane. "A long pull, a strong pull, and a pull both together!"

The party was numerous. It consisted of the two Miss Millions, Sophonisba (*place aux dames,* and, so I put them first;) Caesar Million and captain Shank.

The soldiers had dismissed the boatmen, and for some time pulled at the oars; but weary with tugging, they hoisted the sail, and *hinc illæ lachrymæ!* Hence their danger; hence the shrieks of the females; hence the petitions of Caesar for help.

How unlike the Caesar of antiquity, who called to his terrified boatman, *Quid times? Caesarum vehis! et fortunam Caesaris!*

The boat being righted, lieutenant Hurricane went to the assistance of the eldest Miss Million, who was either fainting, or affected to faint; while Mr Echo still folded Sophonisba in his arms, who reclined her head on his shoulder, as if still imploring the succour of her lover.

Caesar had again taken the helm, and again the boat was up in the wind; the sail flapped against the mast, the girls screamed, and the lap-dog of Miss Million joined his bark in the uproar.

"Jump, Harry!" cried Echo, "and put the helm up."

"My helm," rejoined Hurricane, "is already hard up!"—Miss Million had recovered, and had caught lieutenant Hurricane for safety round the middle.

"Go, sweet!" whispered Sophonisba to young Echo; "go and direct the boat, I beseech you!"

"Come then, and sit next me."

"I will."

Echo now put the boat's head aright, not keeping his eyes off Sophonisba, who had taken a seat next him, and whom he encircled round the waist with his disengaged arm.

Caesar could not conceal his pique. "You need not, sir, give yourself any trouble with *that there* lady. She is engaged, sir, to me. She is under my protection, sir, I say."

"Your protection! Do you carry top or cross-trees above your lower mast-heads?"

"I do not understand your sea-terms. I am, (laying his hand on his heart) I am a military man!"

"So am I, by G——!" cried captain Shank, rising and hectoring.

"Then," said lieutenant Echo, "there is a pair of you!"

"I am a soldier!" responded Shank.

"So am I!" cried Caesar.

"I am a sailor!" vociferated Echo.

"So am I!" bawled Hurricane.

"Say no more now, Caesar," cried Shank, "before the women. We shall find a time! Slugs in a sawpit! Death before dishonour!"

"Don't you bother old sailors!" said Echo, "Miss Sophonisba, you may perceive, will sit next me."

"Will you, Sophonisba?" said Caesar.

"I must, cousin," replied the nymph, "out of gratitude."

"What deceit!" cried Caesar. "Did you not tell me there was something enchanting in a red coat, madam?"

"I did, sir. But I still might have thought a blue coat divine!"

Caesar bit his lip, and whispered Shank in the ear.

"Huzza! Tom!" cried Hurricane. "She is your wife, my sea-officer! Blow my good breeze! Land us on the sod! I will go myself for a chaplain and get you both spliced, before the guard-ship at Spithead shall fire her evening gun!"

It happened that at the place where Mr Echo landed the party, captain Brilliant had come for a stroll with Cassandra and Flora.

"Faith!" exclaimed the captain, "the Miss Millions and Miss Spa! Ladies, your humble servant. Ensign Caesar, how do you do? Captain Shank, I am glad to see you."

"Captain," cried Caesar, "*that there* young midshipman of your's"——

"Midshipman!" roared Hurricane: "he is a lieutenant. Don't you see his wash-boards!"

"That young lieutenant of your's," resumed Caesar, "wants to jockey me out of Sophonisba; But I *vont* give her up. I *vont* be done out of twenty thousand pounds!"

"Then it was not my person, Caesar; it was my fortune at whose shrine you sacrificed the incense of your flattery!"

"All men," rejoined Caesar, "marry for money."

"That's false," cried Echo. "I am a man! and I would take this young lady for my wife, if she had only one shift to her back, and was obliged with that one to make a main-topsail-haul!"

This speech was too much for Brilliant. In his composition the weeping muse had no part. And he now laughed much louder than any of Homer's gods.

"Blast the money!" resumed Echo. "I have more than I know what to do with. I got above five hundred pounds prize-money in the war.—And besides this, I receive a lieutenant's half-pay."

"And you rank, Tom," said Hurricane, "with a captain in the army. You forgot that, messmate."

"Ladies," said Cassandra, "will you do me the honour to visit me at my house. After your excursion you require some refreshment."

The party now walked to the house, where Cassandra received them with such fascinating manners, that all animosity was forgotten, and Caesar and Echo very cordially shook hands. Nay, the ladies agreed to stop and dine, which the soldiers concurred with.

Caesar and Shank were evidently weary. Each threw himself on a sopha and sunk to slumber.

Echo winked to Hurricane, and they withdrew to the garden.

"Harry," said Echo, "did you ever hear of a place called Gretna Green?"

"I have, Tom, it is the port that brings up the runaways. They go there to get spliced."

"Whereabouts is it?"

"I cannot exactly tell; but I think it is in Ireland. However, to be certain, I will go and overhaul my gazetteer."

While Hurricane was gone, Echo walked up and down the garden with disordered pace. A sailor never forgets his quarter-deck step.

"I have made the land, Tom," cried Hurricane, returning. "Gretna Green is in the chops of Scotland. It bears from Chelsea north-west three-quarters north; and it is distant one hundred leagues. With a fair wind you may run it in two days, for the devil's in it, if a post-chaise cannot sail at the rate of six knots an hour. And you was always a h—l of a fellow to carry sail."

"I will carry sail till I run my vessel under water."

"But will Sophonisba shove her boat off with you?"

"Yes; for when I asked her to shove off her boat with me for Gretna, she sighed like the wind when it whistles through a block, and said, Love I will."

"When did you ask her?"

"Why, just after I took that swig at her lips."

"You are a lucky fellow! Sophonisba would, I guess, either sail, scud, or lie-to, better than Flora or Cassandra. She has a noble pair of cat-heads for rousing an anchor up to her bows."

"She is more beautiful than the *Britannia* going large before the wind."

"How nicely she bends her sails!"

"What a clean run she has from her bows all the way to her counter!"

"What a pair of toplights!"

"What head-rails, Harry!"

"You'll be very happy, Tom!"

"She shall go to sea with me, Harry!"

"Go from sea, Tom. You are now both at Chelsea, and will leave it, I do not doubt, before the commodore at Spithead tumbles down the main hatchway."

Chapter 17

AN elegant dinner was provided for the party, and when the ladies withdrew from table, the conversation was unrestrained.

"Shank," said Caesar, "I can neither stand nor sit at ease."

"Whose fault is that?" said captain Shank.

"Why your's," replied Caesar.

"Mine!" rejoined captain Shank.

"Yes!" cried Caesar. "I say, your's! you have made my waistcoat and pantaloons so tight that I undergo torture."

This raised a laugh. It announced captain Shank to be a tailor. But honour and shame, says the poet, from no condition rise. It surely mattered not.

But captain Shank was of a different opinion. He never reasoned abstractedly.

"Caesar," said he, "pray sink the shop when you are in company. You hurt my feelings."

"So did colonel Tub," said Caesar, "hurt mine, when last review he trod upon my toe. He takes up as much room as saint Pauls."

Captain Brilliant circulated the bottle; and being called on for a toast, he gave, "All hearty fellows."

"With aw-all my heart!" hiccupped Caesar, who, now exempt from the restraint of his mother, was in the high road to get fuddled.

"Our bottle is out," cried captain Brilliant. "More wine, hoa!"

"More wine, hoa!" echoed Caesar.

"Ditto!" bawled Shank.

"D—n your ditto!" cried Caesar. "He is still in his counting-house."

More wine was brought; more wine was drunk. Caesar sang the last song he had heard at the opera; it was highly applauded. Shank was called on in succession.—"Haul your wind," whispered Hurricane to Echo. And while captain Shank was chaunting "Jemmy Linkhum Feedle,"—the young lieutenant withdrew.

Brilliant, who divined the motive that actuated young Echo to withdraw, engaged his guests in conversation.

"You must see some duty, gentlemen."

"By G——! sir," cried Shank. "No disparagement to your profession; but, no duty will bear, I believe, comparison with our's. We can call no hour of the night our own; the solemn time of midnight is not sacred. If there is a fire in the parish, the drummers beat to arms! Then such marching and counter-marching. Such ranking and flanking! such bawling to the troops! Close column of the central company face to the rear! Light infantry wheel backward four paces to the left. Left wheel, and form line! Quick march!"

"Ah! bah!" cried Caesar. "Shank! no more parade cant. Get rid of your heeltaps."

When young Echo left the room, he thus soliloquized: Let me now see how the land lies. The ladies are in the drawing-room. I would rather board a hundred of the enemy's frigates, than steer my boat into a fleet of modest women, for a modest woman never fails to take me aback. I can strut up to a blowing as pompous as a midshipman, when the lieutenant leaves him in charge of the deck; but the looks of a modest woman always takes my sails flat aback; my ship has sternway, and I am obliged to shift my helm. If this house was the Jerusalem, or the Anti-Gallican, oh! shins and shank-painters! how soon I would get my anchor a cock-bill! but here,—

In this part of our young hero's soliloquy, a female foot, descending the stairs, suspended his utterance. He looked—it was Sophonisba.

"My angel! Sophonisba!" said the young lieutenant, and stopped.

Sophonisba saw his distress. Her penetration was intuition. She addressed him with the accent of encouragement.

"Silence in love betrays more woe
Than words, however witty;
The beggar that we know is dumb,
Deserves a double pity!"

"That's a proper fine song," said Echo.

"Song!" responded Sophonisba. "It was never designed for music."

"Your voice," returned Echo, "gives it music."

"Oh! how you can flatter!" said Sophonisba.

"Flatter!" rejoined Echo. "I tell you, my angel! by the holy G——, you are—upon my salvation you are——"

"Oh. fie!"

"Sophonisba! I say, will you shove off with me?"

"My dear Echo."

"I say, if you don't consent; I will run and jump overboard."

Sophonisba was silent: but she cast a look of tenderness at Echo, and heaved a sigh.

Echo took down a bonnet that hung at the foot of the stairs. It belonged to Cassandra. But no matter. Sophonisba involuntarily put it on; involuntarily accepted the tendered hand of the lieutenant, and involuntarily hurried with him into the street.

Lieutenant Echo sought a coach, but there was no coach to be had. It signified not. Sophonisba had often danced till midnight at a ball; and admitting these premises, it naturally follows that she could walk or run half a dozen miles with a lover. Her feet did not now fail her; but to town she directed her footsteps, arm in arm with a man who loved her for herself.

Chapter 18

IN about half an hour, Sophonisba was missed by the females in the drawing-room, and Miss Million raised the hue and cry after her. She ran into the room where the gentlemen were sitting.

"Brother! brother! What do you think! Sophonisba is missing! I know where she is gone! I'm certain, sure I know! She's gone with the handsome lieutenant!"—

"Madam," said Mr Hurricane, "you certainly mistake. I am the handsome lieutenant; and here I am before you at an anchor in my chair."

This was too much for the risible muscles of captain Brilliant; he laughed, he stamped, he roared.

"Brother!" resumed Miss Million, "instead of tippling more wine, I think you might go and look for Sophonisba. This will be a pretty tale to be told of one of our family. While you are beating the bush, another runs off with the bird. I know what will be the consequence. Papa will have a return of his gout, and mamma's nervous complaint will come on again. She will have her spasms; I know mama will have her spasms!"

"Let us pursue the fugitives," cried captain Shank, rising from his chair. "Let us make a forced march after them. Let us march to quick time. We shall soon be up with their rear guard."

"Make yourself easy," said Caesar. "The sailor cannot keep Sophonisba, even if he marries her. Sophonisba is under age. Sophonisba is a ward of chancery. Her husband shall be prosecuted for stealing an infant."

"Brother!" cried Miss Million, "how can you talk so! You are more plague than enough. The young man is a sailor; and before this time to-morrow, I dare say he will be in America."

"His ship must sail very fast, then," said Mr Hurricane. "I never heard of so quick a passage before."

The ladies had now all assembled in the room.

"A mutiny!" cried captain Brilliant. "Four women got together in the same house!"

"Be pacified, Miss Million, I entreat you," said Cassandra. "It is a fine moonlight night. They are, perhaps, only gone for a walk."

"No! no!" rejoined Miss Million. "Sophonisba has run away with the young man. Those sailors are such sly fellows; they do not court with fine speeches, but make familiar with you without saying, By your leave. How the lieutenant pulled and hauled our cousin about in the boat! And how the hussey looked at the fellow!"

"Yes! I *see'd* them, sister," said Miss Mary. "It was quite naisty! Brother has no more heart than a mouse, or he would have resented it. I wish I had been a man! Yes, I wish I had been a man."

"I, madam," cried captain Shank, "resented it. I obliquely challenged him. I insinuated that I expected the honour of a meeting with slugs in a sawpit."

"Faugh!" said Miss Million. "You was upon the high stilts at first, but the lieutenant soon took you down."

"Madam," cried captain Shank, "your sex privileges you to talk: but I am sure, no man in company would—ha! hem! well! no matter!"

"More wine!" cried Caesar.

"Brother!" said Miss Million, "are you not ashamed of yourself. You are now more than half tipsy."

"Half tipsy!" cried Caesar: "Indeed I am not ha-half tipsy. Do not think I, I am ha-half tipsy? This is captain Shank. This is my captain. I am not ha-half tipsy. I am a soldier bold! ! !"

"To arms! then!" cried Shank. "To arms! I say! to arms!"

"To arms!" repeated Caesar. "We will all of us to arms!"

The whole family were thus assembled, and all concerting different measures, when such loud and repeated raps were heard at the door, that had it not been formed of strong materials, it would certainly have been knocked down. All ran to the passage. The women expected to behold again the fugitives, and Miss Million with her own hands pulled open the bolt.

But what was her astonishment, when the door was opened, to be caught in the arms of a man, who with an invincible assurance thus accosted her:

"The prettiest house-made I ever saw with my eyes! Ye gods! what a clean run along the bends. Ambrosia and apple-dumplings! what projecting cat-heads! And how she has dressed ship! All the colours of the universe contend for the honour of decorating her rigging! Smack! What lips! They are sweeter than sugar-cane!"

"Tempest!" cried captain Brilliant, "or there are no negroes at Jamaica! Welcome to my house."

"Yes, I have found out your rookery house. But I beg pardon. Mrs Brilliant, your humble servant. Mrs Hurricane, your most obsequious." And here let the imagination of the reader supply many bows, many courtesies, many smiles, and much shaking of hands.

Captain Tempest having discovered his mistake, begged pardon of

Miss Million for his abrupt salutations. "Yet, confess," said he, "upon your conscience, now, (whispering) did you not like it when I was after holding you in my arms?"

"I was never hugged so before," murmured Miss Million.

"No, by Jasus!" said captain Tempest; "because you never had Pat before for a lover."

Tempest was a man of unsubdued confidence. It was not in the power of female modesty to call a blush into his cheeks, or suspend the volubility of his tongue. He was an entire stranger to what my Lord Chesterfield terms *mauvaise honte.*

Captain Brilliant ushered his guests into the parlour. Miss Mary Million had recognised the bonnet of Sophonisba in the passage, and she ran into the room, holding it in her hand.

"Sister!" said she, "you was premature. Sophonisba is not gone. I have found her bonnet."

"Stuff!" cried captain Shank. "All stuff! She is now on the march. She has brigaded herself with the sailor. She is deploying for town. She has changed her position. She is gone to the right about. She has taken up a new line by the echellon movement. Caesar! To arms! Recover, comrade, your arms! Oh! gloomy night! Fall moon and stars! Fulminate, ye heavens! Drop hailstones, ye clouds! Caesar is conquered!"

"That's a good one!" cried the young ensign. "Cae-Caes-Caesar conquered! Don't you discharge your musket before it is loaded! Right centre company right face! By the right counter-march. Remaining companies outward face. Halt! Front! Dress! Column open from the rear! March! Gentlemen, I am not drunk. I can march left foot first. Drums beat up! March!"

"What's all this?" cried Tempest. "I thought I had got to Chelsea; but I find I am at Chatham barracks!"

The evening had now advanced, and the Miss Millions expressed some impatience to get home.

"I know," said the eldest girl, "mamma will have her spasms again, if we don't return soon. Brother, get your hat. We will run up stairs for our bonnets."

"I want coffee!" cried Caesar. "I am dying for a cup of coffee!"

"Then come up into the drawing-room," rejoined the sister. "Leave, leave your filthy wine."

Caesar now ascended into the drawing-room, assisted by the ladies and captain Shank; the naval heroes keeping below, to confabulate without restraint.

Chapter 19

"THE girl I caught hold of," cried Tempest, "is a pretty figure of a female. You may however, discern she was bred east of Temple Bar—she is so d—d ungrammatical."

"That's the misfortune," said Brilliant, "of her education. But I dare say she has good natural parts."

"No matter," replied Tempest; "it always shocks my delicacy to talk with a woman who has more curls to her hair, than grammar in her noddle. By Jasus! the *laist* brogue in a woman always throws me into a *faiver.*"

"I reckon," said Hurricane, "she has plenty of bit."

"Her father," observed Brilliant, "can give her twenty thousand pounds. He is as rich as a jew."

"Ha! ha!" cried Tempest; "say you so? By the hookey, I have a mind to make her a captain's lady."

"She appears," said Hurricane, "to be engaged to a captain already. Shank told me, in secret, after the second bottle, that his father was a rich merchant tailor, and that the old man had held a council of war with Mr Million about splicing him to Miss Million."

"And how soon," cried Tempest, "I would lay an anchor out to windward of the whole boiling. But the girl is so inelegant and ungrammatical. She does not seem to know the four cardinal points of the compass. We should never square our yards together by the lifts and braces. I require an enlightened woman for my wife; a girl of sentiment and liberal accomplishments; one worthy to sail in company with a first rate duchess. How the devil could I take my wife to court, who did not know the main-tack from the captain's epaulet?"

"Very just," said Brilliant. "A refined woman for ever!"

"Oh! refinement is every thing," exclaimed Tempest.

"But a man of your acquaintance," replied Brilliant, "might polish a young wife. Your conversation would insensibly improve her."

"True, very true, my dear fellow," said Tempest. "If the girl had any notion of answering her helm. I would soon cultivate her mind. But if a girl does not learn grammar at school, you would not be able afterwards to beat it into her head with a chisel and mallet."

"You could hire a parson," said Brilliant. "A thousand parsons would jump mast-high at a salary of twenty pounds a year, and to be found in his rations."

"Oh, d—— all parsons!" cried Tempest, "I think it ominous to meet one."

The two Miss Millions, accompanied by the soldiers, now entered the room, wrapped up in their cloaks.

"Arrah! my lasses," cried Tempest; "your fore-topsails are loose, the signal for sailing. But none of you fired a gun."

"Good night, gentlemen," said the ladies.

"Ladies!" cried Brilliant, "before you make sail, let me observe to you, that the coast every night, from Chelsea to Hyde-park Corner, is infested with land-privateers; that after sun-set, robberies and murders are not uncommon."

"Good heaven!" exclaimed Miss Million, "we are in danger of our lives. I will never come out no more after this."

"Fear nothing, my charming fair," said captain Shank, taking the hand of Miss Million. "I am your man! at the crack of your fan, I will defend you with the valour of a man of war. This weapon has never failed me—as the man says in Drury Lane:

> I have seen the day,
> That with this little arm, and this little sword,
> I've made my way through more impediments,
> Than twenty times your stop!

"Confide in my protection! Confide in the protection of a man, whom you love for the dangers he has past, and whose recital of hair-breadth 'scapes in the enemy's deadly breach, won first your maiden heart. Come, my intended! *Allons!* all along! as Monsieur Toupe says."

"Oh! I am scared to death!" said Miss Million. "Captain Brilliant, could I not hire a man to go home with us? I would give him a guinea."

"Here he stands before you!" cried Tempest. "I will take you under my convoy. I have no sword; but I have this little shillela. And if any land-privateer should lay us along-side—by the hook and by crook, I would cut him up in junks."

"Indeed, captain," said Miss Million, "your polite offer sets my heart at ease. Indeed, sir, I am very sensible of your goodness."

"Say not a word, honey," replied Tempest.—"Come, let us fill and be off."

"I will go with you, captain Tempest," said Hurricane, "and guard the other young lady."

"My dear Hurricane!" cried Flora.

"If any land-privateer," resumed Hurricane, "should come

athwart our hawse, I would soon cut his cable."

"Spring your luff, then," cried Tempest. "I will introduce you to Mrs Tempest. She is now leaning sentimentally on her elbow, looking out of the cabin window for me, and dropping a salt-water tear at my absence. Spring your luff, my sea-officer. I will shew you sport!"

"Yes that I believe," said Flora. "Very well, Hurricane: you want to break my heart! You know the state I am in. You will stay out all night."

"Flora!" rejoined Hurricane, "upon the word of a man, I will return to you in a couple of hours: I will, upon my soul."

"That's a dear creature!" exclaimed Flora, in a rapture. "Bye, bye, love!"

"Heave ahead, Jerry! heave ahead!" said Tempest.

Miss Million now took the arm of Tempest, and her sister accepted that of Hurricane. Many adieus were reciprocated, and away the party marched. Caesar and captain Shank bringing up the rear, and vociferating a number of phrases which they had acquired at the drill.

No sooner had the party set out, than satan, or, in language more popular, the devil began to brood mischief in various shapes. The night, awfully dark, facilitated his designs.

The party had walked about half way up Sloane-street, when three footpads attacked them, crying "Give up your money!"

"Yes!" cried Tempest; "I will give it to you;" and so saying, he began vigorously to cudgel them with his shillela. A battle-royal now ensued, in which there was a disparity: for Tempest and Hurricane had to sustain the onset of the three robbers. Where then was captain Shank? Where ensign Caesar? Alas! Shank, with commendable prudence, decamped in search of the watch; and Ceaesar had vanished like a ghost at the crowing of the cock.

But no matter. Tempest and Hurricane very soon dispersed the assailants and prosecuted their walk with the ladies.

The devil thus defeated in one purpose, thought of another that was more likely to be attended with success. He whispered Tempest in the ear, and with irresistible eloquence urged him to run away with the banker's daughter! at the same time insinuating his cloven foot into the heart of the damsel.

"Did I not defend you like a man?" whispered Tempest, in the ear of the nymph, squeezing her at the same time significantly by the hand.

"Oh! you are so brave!" said Miss Million.

"And are you of opinion that none but the brave are worthy of the fair?"

"Indeed I think so."

"Then if I am brave and you are fair, our destiny points to an union. Let us part company from Hurricane and your sister; and before two nights more are over, I will make you a captain's lady."

"My dear captain! what would my papa and mamma say? There would be such a piece of work! I could never look them in the face."

"I will look them in the face for you. Let us alter our course. I will charter a chaise for Gretna-Green."

"Oh, dear! I do so tremble. When Shank offered me marriage, I heard him unmoved; but I declare you make me shake with fear."

"Arrah! honey! cling to my arms! I will be as tender as a turtle dove."

Oh! thou tempter of the human race! whose agency is felt and acknowledged throughout the habitable globe; thou angel of darkness! how camest thou to put it into the head of captain Tempest to whisper the tale of love in the ear of Miss Million, and dispose the nymph to hear it? Alas! no longer does she dread that mamma will have the spasms; her visions are now of a more tender nature.

Chapter 20

LET us now return to lieutenant Echo, and the fair Sophonisba, whom we left together, dancing it away from Chelsea to Hyde-Park Corner. I can now behold the young officer handing the timid maid into a chaise, and the driver pursuing the road that leads towards Scotland. I behold the two pilgrims thus departing at night—not to rob, or to steal, or to betray—but to get to Gretna-Green; a spot more delicious than the feigned gardens of Adonis or Alcinous.

They travelled all night with inconceivable speed; never was there a quicker succession of chaises on the road. But the next morning as they were about to enter the little village of Henley, their chaise broke down, and their flight was impeded.

Had the vessel of lieutenant Echo struck against a rock, he could not have been disposed to swear with more vehemence. I say disposed; for before he could articulate his first oath, the eye, the smile, the whole animated visage of Sophonisba, soothed the transports of his rage! So true is it, that the presence of the fair sex never fails to soften men's manners. *Emollit mores, nec sinit esse feros.*

In this mournful situation, a chaise was discovered behind, scouring furiously along the road, the horses snorting, the dust flying.—Sophonisba turned pale.

"Here they overhaul us!" cried Echo. "Here they over-haul us hand over hand!—But no matter. I am ready for action." And so saying, he put his hand into his pocket, and grasped a pistol, that he had provided for his defence.

The solicitude of Sophonisba very soon subsided. The chaise behind did not contain pursuers, but another tender couple, who were also dancing it away to the hymeneal altar; namely, William Tempest, esquire, late commander of his Britannic Majesty's ship the *Salamander*, and Amelia Million, eldest daughter of Miles Million, esquire, banker, of the city of London.

Miss Million was so wrapped up in a calash and cloak, that Sophonisba, at first did not recognize her; but the dress of Tempest announced him to be a naval officer.

The road was extremely narrow; and the broken-down chaise of the lieutenant, obstructed the passage.

"Chaise, ahoy!" called captain Tempest.

"Hulloa!" said Mr Echo.

"I wish," rejoined Tempest, "you would not block up the gangway in this manner. It is worse than the Straits of Baffleman, where you cannot square your yards for monkeys."

"We are clearing the wreck," cried Echo.

"Dear me!" exclaimed Miss Million, "it is Mr Echo! And, bless me! I now see Sophonisba.—Cousin! Oh! I am so glad to meet you! How do you do, child?" And so saying, she skipped out of the chase to embrace Sophonisba.

"Heavens!" exclaimed Sophonisba, "My cousin Amelia! Where are you going?"

Amelia hung down her head.

"Going!" cried Tempest; "arrah! she is going to the altar before the wind.—She is going to get her marriage-tacks on board."

"If that's the case, sir," said the young lieutenant, "you might as well help us to a passage on board of you. My vessel, you see, is a mere wreck upon the water."

"Come on board," said Tempest. "Let us stow close. My bride, I presume, has no objection to close stowage."

Amelia hung down her head.

"I hope," cried Tempest, "before to-morrow night, to be riding the gale out in a white-limed chamber. Driver! make sail!"

Joyously did our amorous group now jig it away for the temple of hymen; nor did the lovers forbear either glance or toy, with their fair and willing mistresses.

At length they arrive at Carlisle; and now they are within one stage of Gretna-Hall. Fresh horses are ordered, and Echo beheld the structure of Gretna rise to his view with not less transport than the mariner descries land. Their errand was divined by the country people on the road; and they scarcely passed a human face that did not display a broad grin.

The snorting steeds stop at the door of Gretna-Hall. They knew well the place; they had conveyed many a couple thither before. A curly, red-headed, Scotch boy, opens the door of the carriage; the heroes leap out, they take their brides by the hand, and lead them, blushing, but nothing loth, to the chamber of wedlock.

"You boy!" vociferated Tempest.

"Sir!"

"Pass the word for the chaplain!"

"Chaplain, sir?"

"Aye! the parson. Tell him to bear a hand here. We want him to read a page out of Hamilton Moore to us. We want him to splice us. Tol de rol! tol de rol!"

A blush burned in the cheek of Amelia; and the eyes of Sophonisba now sought and now declined the encounter of the young lieutenant's.

While the boy was gone for the blacksmith, the party amused themselves with reading the inscriptions on the wainscot of the room; inscriptions which sentimental minds would have perused with rapture, but which served only to call forth a loud laugh from the lungs of Tempest. I will insert a few of them.

> Who would not renounce the universe for one single tear of love.
>
> Call the blacksmith! Haste! call the blacksmith! for I am sick of love.
>
> Warm as the sun-beam, pure as the driven snows,
> The enamoured youth for sweet Clarissa glows,
> Drops the still tear, with kind attention sighs,
> And woo's the goddess with adoring eyes.

What powerful necromancy there can be in this poetry, I am at a loss to find. Yet the Edinburgh reviewers have pronounced it a very favourable specimen of a brilliant imagination; and, no doubt, it operated upon them like a spell, soothing their souls and lulling them into a voluptuous languor.

Hamlet remarks that, *a man may smile, and smile, and be a villain*! The *Edinburgh Review* has convinced me that, *a man may write, and write, and be a blockhead.*

But enough of Settle! Let us leave the Edinburgh reviewer for a man of more consequence.

Behold the blacksmith, ycleped Parson of Gretna-Green. Lo! he enters the room. What gravity of countenance and solemnity of mien! But see! how he staggers! Wherefore this serpentine motion? Ah! bah! He has only taken his morning glass.

"Hoa!" cried captain Tempest. "Why, I say, Mr Parson; you have been bowsing up your jib-stay! Come, splice this lady and me, and that gentleman and his lady; and then we will take a pull at the halliards together."

"Ring the bell, will you—ring the bell, will you?"

"Yes!" cried Tempest, "I'll ring the bell, and give such a peal, that I'll make all sneer again. But, first, I say, splice us!"

Amelia murmured unintelligibly.

"Pull the bell, will you—pull the bell—the young ladies would like a glass of wine."

"Not any, sir, I thank you kindly," said Sophonisba.

"Come, parson," cried Tempest, "Do your duty."

"Softly!" said the parson. "I always come to terms before I marry.

My price is twenty guineas for each couple. Nor is it much. When Lord Saddog ran away with Miss Wealthy, the banker's daughter, he gave me a hundred pound note for marrying them. I am well known. It was I who married Mr Perry: and I was sent for, at a vast expence, to attend his trial at Bristol. I shall never forget the speech which Erskine made."—

"Well," replied Tempest, "do your duty, parson; I will give you the twenty guineas."

"But, captain," rejoined the parson, "we want somebody to give the young ladies away. Let me see. Joey the postillion, will do for one father, and Sandy the ostler, for the other.—Pull the bell, will you; pull the bell."

The bell was rung, and the boy entered.

"Archibald," said the parson; "tel Joey and Sandy to come hither."

Joey and Sandy were obedient to the call. They entered the room, each grinning, and each scratching his head.

"Joey!" cried Tempest, "we want you to stand father here."

"Yes, measter," replied Joey. "And it bea'nt the first time. It was I who geave awöy madam Wealthy to my Lord Saddog."

"You may tell that to the marines, Joey," said Tempest, "but I'll be d—— if the sailors will believe it. However, no matter. Come, parson, where's your book?"

The parson now proceeded to business.

"Will you have this woman for your wife?" etc. etc.—"Will you have this man for your husband?" etc. etc. To which our naval heroes replied with a sounding "Yes!" and their brides with blushing timidity faultered out the word.

O Modesty! supreme voluptuousness of love! It is thou who givest to woman a fascinating power. It is thou who suffusest her cheek with a blush: it is thou who teachest her bosom to give undulation to the gauze's fold: it is thou who causest her eye now to seek, and anon to decline the encounter of her lover's.

Captain Tempest was now wedded to Amelia, and lieutenant Echo to Sophonisba. The parson's bill was paid; the horses were again put to, and back the bridegrooms and brides were conveyed with rapidity to Carlise. There, in the language of the chaste Milton,

> Their fill of love, and love's desport
> Took largely; of their mutual flame the seal;
> The solace of their souls; till dewy sleep
> Oppress'd them.

Chapter 21

OUR married group remained a week at Carlisle, of whom it may be said, that each couple was one flesh.

Echo was now happy. But the mind of Tempest was susceptible of other energies beside those of the conjugal state. It is true, that he saw and felt that his bride was charming. She had fair hair, languishing blue eyes, a nose somewhat aquiline, and pouting red lips. Her teeth were also good, and she had one of the finest bosoms in the world. These were her charms; but what does the poet say?

> Beauty soon grows familiar to the lover,
> Fades in the eye and palls upon the sense.

Now it is not so with money. Gold is not of that quality, that satiety which must necessarily follow possession. Amelia had other charms than those of person. She had twenty thousand in the care of the directors of the Bank of England; and, in a word, Tempest was secretly jealous that those charms should have any guardian but himself.

The breast of Echo knew not this aching. Content with the possession of Sophonisba, he wanted not to multiply his money. Sophonisba to him was every thing. She was his ship, his yacht, his barge, his pinnace. Indeed she was an exquisite girl. Before marriage she was lovely: but now she was an earthly houri.

Three weeks had now elapsed, when the wedded group returned to London. Tempest took a suit of rooms for his bride in Saint James's; and Echo carried his wife to Chelsea, where they were received with acclamations of heartfelt joy.

Tempest now proposed to his bride to visit her father and mother. "Let us board them," said he, "in the smoke. Writing of letters is all stuff; it is like playing at long bowls. Let us range up alongside of them."

"Indeed," replied Mrs Tempest, "I shall never be able to look mamma in the face."

"Look mamma in the face!" cried Tempest.—"You ought now to carry your peak higher than ever. You are a post-captain's lady: you rank with the wife of a colonel in the army. Your children will have blood! They will have the blood of an officer of the royal navy in their veins." Captain Tempest was no sneak. He was not uxorious. He could with equal facility manage a ship or a wife. *O! si sic omnes!* The same day Tempest conducted his wife to the house of her father. The footman asked his commands."Shew me up stairs, sirrah!" cried he. The voice and mien of Tempest awed the servant into submission; and, contrary to his master's orders, he conducted our pair into the drawing room. Mary Million and Caesar were sitting by the fire. Mary was knitting; Caesar was studying a treatise on fortification. Mary on looking up, ran with emotion to the arms of her sister. They both burst into tears.

"Oh! Amelia!" cried she, "how naughty you have been. Mamma has had the spasms. Her numbness has come on again. And papa has been so afflicted, that he had not appetite at the lord mayor's feast. It was in the papers, Amelia!"

Caesar, sullen as Ajax in the infernal regions, uttered not a word; but offered to withdraw.

"Stripling!" cried Tempest, intercepting Caesar; "where is your urbanity, where your affection? Trifle not with my feelings, or, by the G—d that made me"—

"My dear Tempest," said Amelia, "be calm I beseech you."

"Youth!" resumed Tempest, "go this instant to your sister. Tender her your hand. You wear the dress of a man; shew yourself one."

Caesar did as he was bidden.

"There!" cried Tempest. "Now go to your father. Make him my compliments. Tell him the husband of his daughter, an officer of the navy—a man that dares do all that becomes a man—tell him Captain Tempest desires his company."

"I go, sir," said Caesar.

Some men, says lord Chesterfield, are to be flattered and some threatened into a thing. Tempest understood the last art.

At last Mr Million, accompanied by his wife enter the room. Amelia throws herself at their feet, and prays their forgiveness. The parents relent. They lift their child from the ground, and tenderly embrace her.

"Your name, sir," said the banker, "is, I believe, Tempest?"

The captain bowed.

"Your fame, sir, is not unknown to me. If I mistake not, you were made post, for heading a party of seamen in storming a fort in the West Indies?"

Again the captain bowed.

"In marrying my daughter, sir, you have done me honour. Her fortune is thirty thousand pounds. The whole shall be made over to you with interest, in four quarterly payments."

"Sir," replied Tempest, "your daughter is a fortune in herself. She is virtuous, lovely, amiable! I saw her, and was conquered. She was the first woman that ever made prize of my heart. Many a woman of quality has eyed me with regard; but the shot of their glances never reached me. None but the fire of Amelia's eyes could cause me to strike! To her I hauled down my jack, my ensign, and my pendant!"

Amelia dispatched a glance at Tempest from under her fair eye-lashes, and heaving her beautiful bosom, fetched a deep sigh.

"She is a good girl, captain," said the banker; "and I lament not her destiny. She is your own."

"I thank you," said Tempest. "Nor will you repent the gift. I will take her to court. She shall be introduced to the first-chop mandarines. But first, I must buy a coach for my Amelia."

Amelia looked fondly at her husband.

"Amelia," said Tempest, "I have business at the admiralty; so stay with your family till four, when I will call for you."

Amelia pouted and looked grave.

"She does not like to be from you, captain," said the banker, "but say you will dine here; and then she will accede?"

"I will do myself the honour, sir." And so saying, the captain withdrew, humming the sentimental tune of, "By the deep nine."

Chapter 22

CAPTAIN BRILLIANT having settled his business in town, prepared to depart for Wales, whither Mr Hurricane and his wife, together with Mr Echo and his wife, had also resolved to go.

They employed three chaises, for two of the ladies took up a great deal of room; and they loaded a chaise in the rear, with bread and cold meat, and fruit and wine, that such as were faint on the road might eat and drink, and be glad in heart.

With regard to Tempest, he was not a man disposed to retire into Wales; he loved the city, where he could sport his figure and possessions. Besides he wished much to sentimentalize his young wife; to grammaticise her english, to give her a taste for poetry, and polish into elegance her city awkwardness. And all this he undertook to do himself! Oh! what a delightful task for a husband to cultivate the mind of his wife! To spread before her a rich intellectual banquet! to engraft ideas on her mind, and new combinations of diction on her speech! To excite her natural susceptibility for all the tender charities! Sweet! Oh! Sweet! I now behold Amelia sitting at the same table with Tempest, devouring up his *belles-lettres* instructions with a greedy ear, considering his precepts oracular, and every day acquiring more expression of countenance.

Our party, in their journey to Bristol, took the more circuitous road of Salisbury, desirous to visit that famous city, whose matchless cathedral boasts as many windows as there are weeks, pillars as there are days, and gates as there are months in the year.

It was the day of the mayor's feast, when captain Brilliant entered Salisbury with his wife, and his friends and their wives. The whole city was in motion. The trumpeters were sounding their trumpets at the gates of the council-house. The cooks and cupbearers, obedient to the sound, were running from the kitchens and the cellars, with dishes and bottles in their hands. The whole city was in motion. The mayor, preceded by the mace bearers, and followed by the clergy and corporation, were marching in solemn procession to the house of feasting.

Oh! it was a goodly sight! A detachment of the war-captains were drawn up in the market-place, in battle array, ready to defend their bacon. And the nymphs of the city had clambered to their casements, and thrust their heads into the public street; some gazing at the huge feeders, some casting from beneath their fine eyelashes, glances at the military, and others recognizing among the men of the gown, the preacher, who, in exhorting them to repentance, had inspired them with tenderness.

Much contention was there that day for the uppermost seats at the feast; and many were the salutations and greetings in the market-place. Like the days, too, that were before the flood, there was much eating and drinking.

After a dinner of peace and quietness and loving-kindness, at the white-hart, our naval heroes accompanied their wives in a walk round the city; and while the mayor and corporation were circulating their bottle, the party subscribed twenty-five pound to the half-famished prisoners of Fisherton-jail.

Sophonisba, who, next to her husband loved a book, called at a bookseller's shop in oatmeal-row, where a little man was standing erect behind his counter, clad in a snuff coloured coat, and blowing his fingers to keep them warm.

"Have you any new publications, sir?" said Sophonisba.

"Yes, miss, I have a perfectly new work, on Abstinence from Animal Food."

"Is it popular, Sir?"

"Not, ma'am, in this city."

"I believe you," cried Brilliant. "They were piping to dinner here, just as we luffed round the council-house. I should not like to find the inhabitants in their rations."

Our party passed the night at Salisbury, and early the next morning proceeded to Bristol, where they put up at the grey-hound in broad-mead.

After crossing the little river Severn, a day's easy journey brought our party to Caerfilly, from whence the chaises were dragged by the populace to the house of admiral Roughknot. The worthy admiral, however *unused to the melting mood,* was wholly overcome by the presence of his niece. Nor was Cassandra without emotion. The white arms of beauty leaned on the shoulder of the worthy man: the tears of Cassandra fell fast; sighs issued from her heart.

"Welcome, my child!" cried the admiral. "Welcome to thy home. I forgive thee leaving me! Thou hast married the man who merits thy affection!"

The moon at this interview, was walking through the cloudless sky; the sons of the cottage were pursuing their dreams; and the repose of the night was disturbed only by the bark of the watch-dog.

Yet Fame, swift-winged Fame, flies with unmeasurable speed, by day and by night. The inhabitants of Caerfilly and the neighbouring hills, shook off their nightly slumbers, to welcome the heroes of my page to their hospitable soil.

Sir Hugh Morgan and his family were not long absent. Tears ceased to flow, and all was mirth, and joy, and jubilee. The harp was brought; the Race of Jenkin was played; and the hall resounded with the steps of the dancers.

Chapter 23

THE joy of admiral Roughknot, at the safe return of his niece, and her gallant captain, was unspeakably great.

"Well, now," said the worthy man, "I am content. I am old, very old. I had the command of a line-of-battle ship in Rodney's action with de Grasse, and that is more than twenty years ago. The last flake of life's coil is now reeved through the block of eternity. But it matters not. I only wished to see Cassandra happily spliced, that which is granted me, and I care not how soon my life-lines may go; whether fate snaps them at the standing part, or whether she casts them off, and they run through the sheave."

"My dear uncle!" cried Cassandra, "I hope you will live many years yet, and behold every year bring more happiness, if it is possible, to Brilliant and myself."

"Captain Brilliant," said the admiral, chuckling, "If this, now, should be a boy; I will turn my pond into a punch-bowl, and invite all the people of Caerfilly to bale it out. There shall be feasting for all hands. Every room in the boar's-head, shall hold as many guests as it will stow. The harp shall be set to work. Old age shall recover its youth; and on that day, James Howels shall shake a foot to the music."

"I am certain, sir, in my own mind," said Brilliant, "that it will be a son. It was the keel of a boy I laid down; and he shall be called, sir, after you."

"Good!" said the admiral. "If the young dog emulates my deeds, he will not disgrace His Majesty's navy. I had always a zeal for the service. From the time I went on board the dreadnought, a little midshipman, not bigger than the topsail-sheet knot, till I was made admiral on the East India station, I was never known to fight the old soldier. The doctor never had me on his list, unless, when by drifting, I got athwart the hawse of a fireship. I was never known to skulk, never known to play at tom Coxe's traverse."

Captain Hurricane now entered the room, accompanied by his teeming spouse: and soon after, lieutenant Echo made his appearance, with his tender bride, smiling loves and graces.

It was the hour of breakfast. The footman had brought the urn, and Cassandra was preparing the oriental beverage.

The old admiral rose from his seat at the entrance of the ladies, and handed them respectively to a chair. He then seated himself between them, and with great gallantry complimented them on the beauty of their looks.

"And so, Mrs Echo," said admiral Roughknot, "notwithstanding the vaunted powers of a red-coat, you preferred a true-blue to it. You chose rather to join hand and heart with a lieutenant on half-pay, who had been all his life afloat, than an union with a quill-driver of extensive fortune."

Sophonisba smiled.

"And I am positive, the young lieutenant is one of the happiest men that ever stepped between the stem and stern of a ship. He is never at rest but when he is sitting along-side of you, or has got you in tow."

"And that is my case, too, sir," said Hurricane. "I am never satisfied unless Flora is within hail of me."

"That will do for the marines," said captain Brilliant.

"Yes," said Flora; "but the sailors will never believe it. My husband must not tell that to admiral Roughknot."

"Why, madam," said the admiral, "it is very credible. You are as full of charms as a ship is of ropes."

"So I think, sir," said Hurricane.

"A very poor compliment!" cried Brilliant. "There are only nine ropes in a ship—the rest in stays, back-stays, shrouds and braces."

"It matters not," said Flora, "I am used to this raillery."

"It is a mere trifle in war-time," returned Brilliant.

"Come, ladies," said the admiral, "let us talk of something more important. Whose cook-week is it, pray?"

Brilliant attempted to stifle laughing, but it was wholly out of his power. He stamped, roared, and made the room echo with an honest unsophisticated ha! ha! ha!

"My dear," said Cassandra, "lord Chesterfield says it is not pretty to laugh aloud."

"Not pretty to laugh aloud!" rejoined Brilliant. "Why, it throws off the spleen, helps digestion, and puts the whole system in better trim."

"Ladies," said the admiral, "I beg pardon—but who stands *cater* this week?"

"Permit me, sir," said Sophonisba. "I will be the cateress. What, sir would you relish to-day for dinner?"

"I leave that, madam," replied the admiral, "to your judgment."

"But, admiral," said Brilliant, "if the cook, or, more politely, the *caterix*, does not get her coppers well cleaned, and her meat well towed, is she not to be cobbed? Mrs Echo, you had better keep a sharp look out. Depend upon it, I will be more severe than ever your governess was. I'll take some of your sheathing off."

"Sir," said Sophonisba, "whatever a court-martial adjudges, I must submit to. But do not accuse me before I am guilty."

In this manner would admiral Roughknot converse with the inmates of his hospitable mansion, preserving his wit and humour at an age when other men are prone to moroseness and gloom. No man ever forgets his original profession. The cask retains the flavour of the first liquor which impregnated it. Once a sailor, always a sailor; and the admiral still spoke in the ship idiom, still fetched his comparisons from on board, and still pursued the metaphors of his early youth. Indeed the cup of the old gentleman's happiness seemed now full. His face was ever cheerful, and his smile denoted a serenity of mind, and a freedom from perturbation.

All his wishes had been centred in the felicity of his niece, whom he loved with the warmth and tenderness of a father. That niece was now married to a man who deserved the precious jewel; who had fought his country's battles, and encreased the glory of her flag; who was not leading a life of idleness, but reposing on his laurels; and who, when his Sovereign again required his services, would be one of the first at the post of honour.

Captain Brilliant and his lady accepted the invitation of the admiral, to make his house their permanent abode; but lieutenant Hurricane and young Echo, having well considered the affair, hired, for a twelvemonth, a ready furnished lodgings in the neighbourhood of Swansea.

Before, however, the gallant tars undertook their journey, they contributed by their hilarity, to the celebration of an event which encreased the happiness of Brilliant.

The lady of this illustrious officer was safely delivered of a son, the pledge of pure and chaste affection.

Before I describe the journey of the two lieutenants towards Swansea, it will be no undelightful task to exhibit the festivity which reigned under the roof of the admiral, when Cassandra was sufficiently recovered to receive the company of her friends.

In the rustic masquerade given by the admiral to the inhabitants of Caerfilly, there were marshaled the gayest groups of a fairy land. The park and gardens of the naval chief were transformed into a kind of enchanted ground, where the inebriate mob, to the soft music of the harp, drenched themselves in the cup of joy.

To the sound of martial music was opened the masquing scene;

and old age, as if feeling a rejuvenescence, exclaimed to the melting fair, in the language of a festive bard,

> Braid you locks with rosy twine,
> Dropping odours, dropping wine;
> Rigour now is gone to bed,
> And Advice with solemn head,
> Strict Age and sour Severity,
> With their grave saws, in slumber lie.
> We that are of purer fire,
> Imitate the starry quire,
> Now to the moon in wavering morris move.

This *fête* was directed by the taste of the admiral. The industry of the town of Caerfilly, formed the vanguard in the army of pleasure, and had long since given pleasing "note of preparation."

The whole host of tailors, mantua-makers and milliners, had been for a month in requisition. Books, painters, carpenters and confectioners, were levied *en masse*, to commemorate the happy day.

To the capacious means which the regular establishment of the admiral's house afforded, were added several temporal accommodations. Of these one was a long and beautiful green walk, extending from the great door of the mansion, in various directions, through an ample and cultivated garden. It was covered in, and hung with numerous festoons of varigated lamps, and terminated by a transparency of a female figure, representing Peace ascending to heaven, after having destroyed War, and his officious fiends. The finest flowers of almost every species, blooming in beds along the sides of the walk, rose in great abundance; while the most beautiful shrubs waved their branches to the soft breeze of night, and mingled their odours. This walk was rendered peculiarly grateful from the freshness of the air, the coolness of the ground, and the fragrance of the flowers; and consequently afforded a happy retreat to all who, in the course of the night, suffered from the heat of the ball room, and interior apartments.

About eight in the evening the company began to assemble, and there was no family of opulence within twelve miles of Caerfilly, that did not hasten to the spot.

Sir Hugh Morgan appeared in the costume of Fluellen, the brave and loquacious Welchman in *Henry the Fifth;* and his accent was highly appropriate, and exquisitely shrewd. The eldest son of the worthy baronet supported the character of a blind Welch harper, and touched the strings of his instrument with no contemptible skill.—Mr Jones personated a landlord of a country inn, with characteristic drollery, and dilated on the commodiousness of his rooms, the abundance of his larder, the excellence of his wines, and the obliging temper of his wife, to the universal mirth and jollity of his hearers.—Captain Morgan acquitted himself with great adroitness in the part of a female barber, a profession common in Wales; and boasted very eloquently of the softness of his soap, and the keenness of his razors.—Colonel Williams, was a Turk of solemn and dignified mien; and the dress of the follower of Mahomet was magnificent beyond description.—Major Parry, lieutenant Evans and Mr Ellis, horse-dealers.—Mr Ownes, was a corncutter.—Captain Hardy personated a jew.—Old Mr James Howels was dressed in the habit of a dutchman; and he acted up to the character, by smoking his pipe and drinking his gin, the whole night. He was, indeed, the most natural character in the whole group.—Mr Philips was in a domino.—Of the domestic group, I shall be allowed to speak minutely.—The admiral personated the character of a Chelsea pensioner, a most excellent mask.—Captain Brilliant appeared as a waterman, and his muscular form and limbs, were well adapted to the character.—Lieutenant Hurricane came forward as Neptune, attended by Mr Rcho as his barber: they acquitted themselves admirably, and provoked considerable laughter.

We now come to the ladies. It would be impossible for the coldest imagination to describe the *ensemble* of this party, without giving an air of extravagance to the picture. Fancy might have regarded the spot as the temple of beauty, where some second Charles had enshrined the loveliest women of the age, as the proudest record of the glory of his reign.

In this most interesting circle, there was a group of fairy queens, composed by the three fair daughters of sir Hugh Morgan, whose ravishing forms excited admiration.—The lovely Miss Williams appeared as an *angel*, dress, white, blue scarf and wings.—Mrs Morgan personated a ballad-singer, and warbled sweetly several ballads of her own composition. Our little song in particular, was loudly encored.

The jutting rocks, the ocean laves,
And soon or late the rocks decay,
Until, with liquid shocks, the waves
Sweep every rugged stone away.

Not so the sea of tears I pour;
Ah! cruel while for thee I pine:
Those seas of tears but harden more
That unrelenting heart of thine.

These verses, sung with corresponding plaintiveness of voice, had a wonderful effect upon the audience.—Miss Evans, the gay, the beautiful and accomplished, was a gipsy, who told fortunes with great archness. She belonged to a group of gipsies, who had pitched their tents, lighted a fire, and put on their pot to boil. They had an ass, with panniars and two fine chubby children of the Egyptian breed. Many a credulous fair one resorted to these oracles, to learn their destinies; and many a specious promise was held out of future lovers, husbands, and numerous progeny.—The lovely Sophonisba was the *chief sibil*, who warbled, with exquisite grace, a wild and original catch

> Where poplars high waving in air,
> Embower the pool,
> We duly at noon-tide repair,
> For quiet and cool.
>
> And do not old Brindle or Pie,
> From the midst of the dell,
> Now tell ye the gipsies are nigh,
> By tinkling her bell?

When the plaudits, raised by this simple unaffected ditty, had ceased, Miss Evans sweetly sung.

> Now eye we the glance of a star,
> Arise in the west,
> To gleam o'er the dell, where afar,
> We seek our night's rest.
>
> By the tinklings and brayings more near
> Our haunt is betrayed,
> And slowly the gipsies appear
> From under the shade.

Of the female masks, the lady of captain Hardy, and her sister, were flower-girls: but it would be an endless task to enumerate every character assumed;—Mrs Brilliant was in an elegant embroidered white-and-silver dress, attended by Flora, in white satin and perls.

The dances commenced about one, and the goddess of the fantastic toe was successful in her inspirations. Reels and strathspeys were danced in true style. The band belonged to the Monmouthshire militia, and more animating music was scarce ever heard.

At three the company sat down to a magnificent supper, and it was broad day before they had made their congratulations to captain Brilliant, and called for their carriages.

I have been the more explicit in describing this scene of fashionable gaiety, because every one, as Doctor Goldsmith says, however low-minded himself, delights to read of high life, and high-lived anecdotes, and memoirs of lords, ladies and knights of the garter.

Chapter 24

IT was at an early hour of the morning, that the two lieutenants and their lovely spouses, bade adieu to admiral Roughknot and their shipmates, captain Brilliant and his lady, and began their journey to Swansea.

It was in the fulness of life and self-enjoyment that our party set out. Their spirits predisposed to cheerfulness, and susceptible of agreeable emotions, shed a brightness on every surrounding object, on hill and dale, forest and plain. Their feelings rendered the murmurings of the rivulet, the rushing of the distant torrent, and the wild music of the woods, a feast of pure, rational and exquisite delight.

The heart of Sophonisba danced with secret gladness. She loved retirement, but she loved an ardent lover in whose ear she could tell the pleasures of retirement, either in the morning, on the mountain-top; at noon, in the shade; or at evening before the door of her modest villa. Such a lover she now found under the endearing name of husband, a husband wholly devoted to her, as the fairest being in creation.

Not being restricted with regard to time, but free as the air of heaven, the party took a circuitous route to Swansea, desirous to visit in their journey whatever was remarkable in nature or art.

A few hours travelling brought them to *Pont y Prid*, that is, New Bridge. This bridge is composed of a single arch, whose span is considered the greatest in the world. It exceeds that of the Rialto in Italy.

This bridge crosses the river Taafe. A little higher up is a famous salmon-leap, but the party, in visiting it, could discover no fish.

Having dined at the bridgewater-arms, an inn, delightfully situated on the road, the party, in charming spirits, prosecuted their journey, and reached Merthyr late in the evening.

To behold the town of Merthyr to advantage, it should be entered at night. For what can be conceived more awfully grand than numberless volcanoes vomiting smoke, and furnaces emitting their vivid lights, till the whole country appeared in flames.

The next morning the gentlemen went to inspect an enormous over-shot wheel, composed entirely of cast iron. It is fifty feet in diameter, and seven feet broad.

This wheel, in an obscure country, deservedly excites attention. It works many inferior wheels, distributing the air with incredible force through different tubes to the furnaces.

From Merthyr the party pursued the road to Cardiff, a very neat town, affording good accommodations.

At Cardiff they stopped to dine, and proceeded to Cowbridge, a town composed of a single street; and where, there being little or no trade, the shopkeepers are continually standing before their doors.

Sophonisba feeling a slight indisposition, her gallant husband ran for the physician, and doctor Bates had the honour of feeling her pulse, and prescribing her regimen.

Doctor Bates is the most intelligent, and the best humoured man, at Cowbridge. But he is troubled with a gouty affection in his legs, which causes him to walk like a person in fetters.

From Cowbridge the party journeyed forward to Pyle House, a solitary but commodious inn on the road. In their way to it, they passed through Neath, a suffocating place, tolerable only to the cyclops. Its venerable abbey is inhabited by the ragged and dirty families of the workmen employed at the copper smelting-houses.

Our party were much pleased with Pyle House, and Mr Marment's family. His two eldest daughters are comely, well-bred, and amiable girls.

The next day, proceeding on their tour, they reached Swansea, from whence it was only three miles to their mansion.

Servants had been already hired to prepare the rooms for the reception of our gallant tars. And it was with no small pleasure that they took possession of their castle.

No house could be more happily situated. It was built on an eminence, and commanded the prospect of mountains, on whose grassy sides the goats were browsing in peace; while through their openings was to be seen the blue expanse of the sea, on whose surface the tall bark was urging her course. Sometimes the water was smooth as a mirror; when it reflected the colour of the heavens above. Upon the springing up of a breeze it changed to a light blue, which deepened to a fine sky colour, as the wind increased—saddened to a deep green in a brisk gale—and in a storm, to a sullen blackness, save where the waves interspersed with white heads of foam, added magnificence to the scene.

There is, perhaps, no man who does not image to himself some future period, when retired from the cares and irritations of his profession, he shall enjoy in the bosom of retirement a freedom from all solicitude.

It was now that era in the lives of our gallant tars. No longer were they summoned on deck by the shrill pipe of the boatswain; no more did the beat of the drum announce an enemy was near; but, to appropriate the words of the song, they *sported on down beds*, or, in language more classical, reposed on roses.

They had not taken possession of their house a fortnight, when Mrs Hurricane presented her husband with a daughter: and the protuberance of Sophonisba denoted she was in a fair way to fulfil the great precept given to the parents of all mankind. In the mean time, their hours were passed in cheerfulness and peace. Sophonisba loved the country, and delighted more in flowery fields than the paved streets of the town. In her retirement she was gratified by a visit from Mr and Mrs Million, together with their son Caesar, and a young lady whom he had led to the altar of hymen. They were making an excursion into Wales, being at a loss how to fill up their time.

Caesar presented his spouse to Sophonisba, and the rest of the family. She was the daughter of an opulent haberdasher, and had captivated the heart of Caesar as she one day sold him a pair of gloves, behind her father's counter. Her age was about nineteen; her person tolerably good, but the structure and phraseology of her sentences denoted that her education was illiberal, and that her reading had been confined to the trash of a circulating library. Yet, in intellect and attainments, she was at least equal to her husband.

"Well, captain Echo," said Caesar, "you see, the preference which Sophonisba gave to you, did not *totally* break my heart. I was, to be sure, a little down in the mouth at first. But when I saw Nancy, my heart recovered its jollification, and I took her for a wife, while I found her in the humour to have me."

"I give you joy, sir," said the lieutenant. "I dare say, you are both very happy."

"We be, indeed, sir," returned Caesar; "*aren't* we, Nancy?"

"Yes," cried Nancy; "when you behave yourself properly. But if ever you call me extravagant again, as you did coming along, in the *chay*, I'll give you no rest for a month. Marry! it is a pretty work to come to this. To call me extravagant, because I bought a pair of ear-rings. Men in general delight to see their wives smart, but you"—

"How long, sir," said lieutenant Hurricane, "have you been married?"

"Almost a month, sir," said Caesar.

"I give you both joy," rejoined the lieutenant.

"Joy! sir," said Nancy. "He'll neither give me joy nor rest. He is more plague than enough!"

"Hush! Nancy," said Caesar. "*Aren't* you ashamed?"

"I won't hush," said Nancy. "Where there is no sin, there is no shame. But I will waste no more words with a poor mean fellow that could begrudge the wife of his bosom the cost of a *gownd.* I am sure he can set no store by her."

"Indeed, Nancy," said Caesar, "I do set great store by you. If you want a hundred pounds you shall have it."

"Very liberal, sir," said Hurricane. "Come, never mind your wife; leave her with my wife, and Echo's wife. Let us splice the main brace. Let us drink some grog together. Come! heave a-head. How do you like my new ship? What think you of the officers' cabins?"

"Nancy," said Caesar, "I am just going to have a little *jollification* with the lieutenant. I shall soon be back."

"Your absence," cried Nancy, "is more welcome than your company. A good riddance!"

Caesar retired with the two lieutenants into their banquetting-room, leaving Mr and Mrs Million, together with his own wife, to walk down the garden, and contemplate the sea.

There are many of my readers (particularly those west of temple-bar) who will consider it very vulgar to drink grog before dinner. But our sailors knew none of this fastidiousness, and never imposed upon themselves the restraints of fashion. They loved grog at sea, and they loved it too on shore.

A bowl of grog was made by lieutenant Echo, and jovially pushed around.

"Come, Hurricane," said the young tar, "sing us a song. You have a good voice?"

"I have no objection to sing," said Hurricane; "and I will give you a song I never heard before. I bought it for a halfpenny, of the ballad-singer, at the admiral's masquerade. It is called

THE HONEY-MOON

Serene and tranquil was the night,
  The night that closed the summer's day;
And brilliant shone the moon, and bright,
  And warm and tender was her ray.

"How like our love!" the husband cried,
  As on his arm Louisa hung:—
Scarce had Louisa been a bride,
  And both were fond, and both were young.

"This moon, how like our love, my dear,"
He said, and clasped her round the waist;
"'Tis pure and perfect, and sincere,
Tender and true, and warm though chaste."

Time flew—the youthful pair again
Enjoyed at eve the stilly vale;
The moon still shewn, but in the wane,
Her form less round, her face more pale.

"This too is like our love, my queen,
For though less radiant and less bright;
Yet still o'er all this sylvan scene,
She sheds a soft and pleasing light."

Louisa bowed her beauteous head,
And yet a sigh escap'd her breast;
Perhaps the fair one would have said,
She lik'd the first bright moon the best.

Time linger'd; yet again the pair
The balmy breath of eve imbib'd,
And now less perfect, yet still fair,
The moon, alas! two horns described.

"This too is love!" Louisa says,
"The love, my dear, that life adorns;
Perfect at first, it soon decays,
Decays and ends, at last in horns."

These stanzas sung with corresponding archness of voice and gesture, provoked the laughter of Echo, and forced a smile from Caesar. The glass went round, more songs were sung, and they were high in mirth, when the footman summoned them to dinner.

I pass over the conversation at the dining table. The whole party were very cheerful, and Mrs Million spoke in raptures of Wales—the high mountains she had ascended—the old castles she had explored—and the romantic prospects she had seen.

They passed another day under the roof of their friends, when they departed for Milford Haven; purposing to return home by the route of North Wales.

The lieutenants were not a little pleased at the unexpected visit of the banker and his lady. Sophonisba had always a respect for the old lady, by whom she had been treated with maternal tenderness; and there is something in the face of an old friend that always makes it welcome.

We may now consider our gallant tars and their wives in their rural privacy, possessed of as much happiness as falls to the lot of humanity. The retrospect of their former days brought with it a self-approving conscience; and the horizon of their future life was gilded with sunshine, giving them assurance of health, and peace, and competence.

FINIS.

Glossary & Notes

CHAPTER ONE

Top lights Signal lanterns placed high in the mast. Used here with reference to his beloved's eyes.

Cat heads Strong beams projecting either side of the bows to which the anchor was hauled up. Here a reference to the lady's bosom.

Sheep-shank Knot used to temporarily shorten a length of rope.

Driver Fore and aft sail carried on the mizzen mast. Was known as the spanker in later merchant square riggers.

Ring-tail Extra sail set abaft the driver in light weather.

Spritsail Small square sail carried on a yard beneath the bowsprit.

Sprit-topsail Smaller additional sail to the spritsail set under the jib-boom.

Royals The sails next above the topgallant sails, fourth in ascending order from the deck.

Skyscrapers Small triangular sail set high aloft to catch every breath of wind in light airs.

Flying jib and jib of jibs The two outermost of the jibs (headsails) set on stays above the bowsprit and jib-boom.

Knots Still the term used for denoting the speed of a ship. Before modern instruments this was ascertained by counting the number of spaced knots which ran out in a given time on a line streamed astern. Today knots means "nautical miles per hour" and to say "knots per hour" is regarded as incorrect, but in earlier centuries experienced officers wrote both terms indiscriminately.

Quartermaster Title used at that time for an assistant to the Master of the ship. The Master was then a warrant officer doing what would now be the duties of the navigating officer.

Top-men Men sent to work sails on the upper yards, usually the best seamen.

Cape fly-away An illusion of land in the distance, such as a bank of cloud.

Afterguard Men allocated to work the sails in the aftermost part of the ship, mainly the less experienced hands.

Weekly account gentlemen Slang term for midshipmen arising from the distinctive white patch on their uniform lapels which presumably looked like weekly account slips.

Boatswain Warrant officer responsible for all upper deck work and sail handling. (Always pronounced "bosun").

Master at arms Warrant officer responsible for all discipline and small arms drill.

Idlers Such people as cooks, sailmakers, etc. who did not normally stand watches but were called when "all hands" were needed.

Loblolly boys The ship's surgeon's assistants. Named after a sort of gruel often prescribed for a sick man's diet.

The people "The people" was one of the commonest 18th and 19th century expressions for what would later be called "the ratings" or "the lower deck". Officers were much more likely to write in letters and reports of "the people" than of "the men" or "crew".

Seven bells Ship's time was kept by watches of four hours divided into half hour periods marked by the sounding of the ship's bell, one stroke for each half hour. Seven bells could signify half an hour before the end of any watch (except the dog watch which differs).

Hammocks were piped up Hammocks were brought from below to be stowed in nettings along the sides of the upper deck where they acted as protection from enemy fire in action.

Purser At this period a warrant officer who was a mixture of paymaster, housekeeper and secretary.

Ground-tier butt A barrel stowed right at the bottom of the hold.

Round house Slang expression for the officers' convenience. Others had to use the windy space right forward known as "the heads" which has become the name by which lavatories at sea are known to this day.

Taken aback Literally for a ship to be caught with the wind dangerously on the fore side of the sails. Commonly used as seamen's slang for "taken by surprise".

Box your ship off To bring the ship on course again.

Making dead men chew tobacco Refers to the sharp practise of keeping the names of dead men on the books to continue drawing their allowances.

Timberhead Projecting post to which ropes could be made fast.

Chelsea Battersea . . . Marshalsea First two names in the lieutenant's very poor pun are places at that time near (now part of) London. The third is less kind. Marshalsea was a debtors' prison.

Waist Midships part of the deck between the quarterdeck and the forecastle.

Topsail-sheet Rope for controlling the set of the topsail.

Lee-lurch Violent roll to leeward caused by a heavy wave striking the windward side.

Kettle Any deep cooking utensil, not necessarily the sort with a spout for which we use the term today.

Burgoo Kind of porridge served with dreadful monotony to seamen throughout the sailing ship era.

Ship's coppers Large pans in which the men's food was prepared in bulk.

Hawbuck Country bumpkin.

All standing Used here to signify gone to bed in his clothes. Properly used of a vessel brought to a sudden stop by her anchor while still moving ahead with sails set.

Banyan day A day when no meat was served, derived from a Hindu word. But banyan was, confusingly, also a naval expression for a picnic or treat.

By the glass Sand glass used to mark the half hourly divisions of the watch.

Gun-room Where the small arms were stored and used as the officers' mess in a frigate. In a ship of the line it was the midshipmen's mess.

Vauxhall Fashionable pleasure gardens for dining and entertainment in London.

CHAPTER TWO

Bulkhead Dividing wall or partition below decks.

Locks Flint locks to fire the cannon were just coming in to replace the old slow match.

Carronade Short, stubby kind of cannon useful for close engagements. Takes its name from the iron foundry on the River Carron in Scotland where it was first made around 1780.

The gentlemen Midshipmen were often referred to as "gentlemen" or "young gentlemen". They were obliged to keep logs and make navigational calculations for the captain's inspection.

Quarter gallery Space between the cabin and the ship's side, usually used as the captain's private walking space.

Jolly-boat General purpose ship's boat, usually with six oars, carried in davits at the stern.

Seventy-four Man o'war with 74 guns.

Salt junk Very old salted down beef or pork.

Studding-sails Sails for extra speed in light weather, rigged by extending the length of the yards by running out a boom through rings at the yardarms. The pronunciation is "stuns'l".

Fore tack Rope used to trim the lower foremost corner of a square sail. To secure it to the cat head would bring the sail hard in while the ship was close hauled.

Weather Adjective applied to anything on the side of the ship on to which the wind is blowing. The opposite is lee.

Clue-garnet More usually spelled clew. A tackle to furl the lower square sails.

Preparations made for action When a man o'war went into action considerable amounts of below deck fittings like partitions, cabins and furniture were dismantled and stowed in a matter of minutes, there being plenty of labour available to do it.

Chains To prevent the yards crashing to the deck if the rigging normally securing them was shot away.

Heavy tier of teeth A long row of guns.

Tompions Circular plugs of wood covering the muzzles of the guns when not in use.

Private signal Recognition flag which required a specific flag hoisted in response to denote a friend, the equivalent of a password ashore.

Jonathan Then current slang for any United States citizen.

CHAPTER THREE

Companion ladder Leading from the quarterdeck to the upper deck, which was the first deck below (i.e. not in the open).

Taffarel Modern spelling "taffrail", a rail round the stern of the ship.

Parbuckle A rope sling for hauling up or securing a heavy object.

Panado An invalid broth made from bread boiled to a pulp and flavoured.

Purser's shirt on a handspike Meaning to say his coat hung on him loosely. A purser would be presumed to be fat by reason of his calling and thus have a big shirt. A handspike was a lever for shifting the position of the guns.

Double cape horn To have sailed round Cape Horn. To sail round any large headland was to "double" it, but it is obviously meant in some derogatory sense here. One commentator suggests it means cuckold.

Sew him up in his hammock Bodies were sewn into hammocks weighted with shot for burial at sea.

Over the standing part of the mainsheet To go over the standing part of the mainsheet was an expression for being buried at sea.

Better Landfall In the real sense a landfall is the first land sighted after a voyage from which an exact position can be established. The Captain's implication is that he hopes to take the lady somewhere better than to tea.

Eating haliards A purely invented bit of buffoonery, playing on nautical words.

Raked fore and aft To be straddled by enemy gunfire from stem to stern, but meaning here to be captivated by Flora's charms at the tea table.

Hate to see a priest It was a common sailors' superstition that clergymen aboard were unlucky. Well into the 20th century fishermen would sometimes refuse to sail if they passed a priest or a nun on the way to the boat.

Tell that to the marines Still a common expression of disbelief. It arose because the seamen thought the marines (i.e. soldiers of the Royal Marine Regiment raised in 1664 to serve with the fleet) were inferior in nautical knowledge and so could be taken in by tall stories.

By the peak of her mizen That is, by her appearance. Comes from the fact that sailors could often identify another ship at a distance by the set of her sails.

Moon-raker Another fine weather sail set above the skysail.

Board the beef in the smoke A reference to boarding an enemy ship under cover of gunsmoke.

This bottle is a marine It is empty. Another derogatory sailors' view of the soldiers.

The lights . . . are put out . . . A serious remark. Brilliant is remembering his responsibilities. As gunpowder is being handled all naked lights must be extinguished.

Avast An order to stop or cease.

Luff-tackles A powerful purchase employing several blocks to tighten the luff (leading edge) of a sail or for general lifting jobs.

Under the lee of In the shelter of.

Marlinspike A spike used for parting strands of rope when splicing. In a similar land phrase Brilliant might have said "He looked at me daggers drawn".

The wind that blows . . . etc. A popular toast at sea, turned into a song by Charles Dibdin.

By goles Expression dating from Chaucer's time meaning roughly "you've said a mouthful". Not connected with the modern expression "by golly" which has a different origin.

Another pull, etc. Reference to a pull on the oars.

Cap Wooden fitting joining the lower and topmasts.

Light out cheerly Carry the rope out vigorously.

CHAPTER FIVE

Humble come-tumble . . . etc. A bit of nautical foolery playing on the "humble servant" mode of address of fashionable society.

Oakum Old rope unpicked to small shreds for caulking decks. The oakum is stuffed between the seams and covered with hot pitch to make them watertight.

Take me with you to sea Even in wartime it was not unusual for 18th/19th century Captains to be given permission to take their wives to sea. It is to the diaries kept by Betsy Freemantle while sailing with her husband that we owe many sketches of Nelson's fleet. Married commissioned and warrant officers were sometimes allowed to take their wives to.

CHAPTER SIX

Mantua maker By this period the word meant any dressmaker, not confined as originally to mantuas which were silk gowns.

New Ferry Passage Before either the present rail tunnel or road bridge crossed the River Severn between England and Wales there were two ferries, an ancient one at the village of Aust and the new ferry referred to here at Portskewet.

Whip Ladies and infirm visitors were taken aboard in a chair hoisted with a rope run from one of the yards and known as a whip.

Coxswain Helmsman in charge of a boat (pronounced cox'n).

Barge A ship's boat, usually pulling 14 oars, often reserved for the conveyance of the captain.

Point Portsmouth Point, the waterfront and place of embarkation.

Astonishment at the uproar Astonishment is a bit of an understatement and out of character even for a light novel. As to this day every coming aboard of the captain would be attended by a "side party" greeting him with salutes, pipes and silence.

Joes West Indian gold coins.

Get the ship under weigh According to the best modern authorities it is correct to say that you "weigh" (i.e. raise) the anchor in order to get the vessel "under way" (i.e. moving through the water). As the two words sound the same though spelt differently it is not surprising that they were confused. They still are.

Devil to pay and no pitch hot Has become a proverbial expression for a difficult problem with no immediate solution. The "devil" was a seam low down near the keel which was difficult to "pay" (i.e. caulk by filling with oakum and a covering of hot pitch).

Bow chaser Light guns fired through the forward ports when chasing an enemy.

Make the clues strand The clues (now usually "clews") are the cords by which a hammock is suspended at each end. To strand a rope is to break one or more strands of it.

Lowering my top-gallant-sails These sails were sometimes lowered as a form of salute between ships. (Always pronounced t'gallant).

Right tack Best course.

Laying an anchor out to windward Used here in the sense of getting the better of, or seizing an advantage. A sailing vessel would lay out an anchor to windward so that she could haul up to it and be in a better position to sail off clear of the shore or other obstruction to leeward.

Plato-comic Malapropism for platonic.

Blue-posts The Blue Posts was a fairly common inn name of the period.

Luff up Bring the ship's head closer to the wind.

Bear away Opposite of luff up. To bring the wind more on the beam, a faster point of sailing.

Stocks and flucke The two principal parts of an anchor. Modern spelling is "fluke".

Reads the articles of war The articles of war are the official regulations governing naval discipline and had to be read by the commanding officer to the ship's company at regular intervals and in such an eventuality as an incipient mutiny, equivalent to reading the Riot Act ashore. These days, when even sailors can read, the articles of war are simply posted up.

Falls were manned Falls were the ropes used to hoist the boats aboard, one being affixed bow and stern. The two ropes were then "married" together and all hands "walked away" with them, bringing up the boat quickly and on an even keel.

CHAPTER EIGHT

Spithead The mile wide stretch of water between Portsmouth and the Isle of Wight, a famous anchorage for the British Navy.

Capstern bars Archaic spelling of capstan, the large cylindrical drum on the forecastle by which the anchor was raised. The bars were inserted like long spokes so that large numbers of men could push the capstan round.

Cast The ship's head paid off so that the sails filled and she gathered way.

Bringing your anchors home In the literal sense refers to anchors that are not holding, but in this context Brilliant perhaps means she will be sea-sick.

Pudding bags Contemporary navy slang for the courses, the lowest and largest square sails.

Evening gun Probably a signal so that all ships in the anchorage could observe sunset colours in unison.

There goes the commodore down the main hatchway All searches have failed to reveal the meaning of this expression and it has not been encountered in any other writings. It obviously is not just a reference to a senior officer going below.

Cot A bed with sides, suspended like a hammock and used by officers.

Laid the keel Laying the keel is the first move in building a ship. Here it signifies Mrs. Hurricane is pregnant.

Quarter-deck step Naval officers had, and still have, a distinctive quick walk when pacing the deck, a manner accentuated by the short space available before they must turn.

Nice sea-boat Term given to any vessel which is sea-kindly and handles well.

Neither stay, nor wear, etc. Ship handling terms indicating a vessel not manoeuvring well, but here meaning the lady will not do her husband's bidding.

Privateer A privately owned armed ship officially licensed by the Government to seek and capture enemy shipping for which they received prize money. They were not popular with the Navy at this time and the practise was abandoned by international agreement in 1856.

Watch and watch Do duty four hours on, four hours off.

Middle watch Midnight to 4 a.m. Sometimes referred to as the graveyard watch.

Main top Platform at the top of the mainmast. As Mrs. Hurricane would hardly be there the reply is a facetious one indicating he doesn't know or care where she is.

Sheet anchor The second or spare anchor.

Which way the ship's head is What compass course to steer, a piece of information every officer of the watch reports to his relief.

Anchor a cockbill, etc. When the anchor is suspended from the cathead held only by the stopper and ready to let go. The shank painter secures it to the side when it is in the stowed position.

CHAPTER NINE

Becket Properly a small rope sling. Used here as slang for pockets.

Fore-mast man Common sailor.

Slack in stays Used of a ship that is sluggish in going about when tacked.

Handsomely In naval language the word means steadily or gently.

Out of soundings Well away from land in deep water.

Shifting backstay Extra backstay (mast support) used when the ship is hard pressed and capable ofbeing moved to the windward side with each change of tack.

Square the yards etc. The captain is joking about the impending marital squalls of the Hurricanes rather than giving directions to his lieutenant about snugging the ship down for rough weather.

Log The device for measuring the ship's speed.

Sheave The wheel over which the rope runs in a block.

Blue jacket This term now means any seaman rating of the Royal Navy but did not come into general land use until 1858 when lower deck uniforms were introduced. Before then it was used on board, as here, to distinguish between a competent seaman and an unqualified hand such as a marine.

Start the main top men To "start" was to hit men with a rope's end to hurry them up. It was the job of the boatswain's mates to do this whenever speedy obedience to orders was required, in fact almost routinely.

Star-bowlines For watchkeeping purposes crews were divided in two parts, named for convenience the "starboard" and "larboard" (later changed to "port") watches. Star-bowlines was a familiar term for the starboard watch.

Old men of war's men Veterans. Not all 18th century midshipmen were boys. Some never passed for lieutenant and remained middies into middle age. Midshipman Culmer aged 49 held the record in 1791, but was beaten in 1822 by Midshipman Vallock, aged 65.

Stood two calls Stayed in their hammocks till the last possible moment.

Dog-vane A light tell-tale made of cork and feathers placed on the rail near the helmsman to show the wind direction in a fickle breeze.

Granny's knot An insecure, unseamanlike knot.

Bob stay Rope from the stem near the waterline to the forward end of the bowsprit.

Blowings Slang for prostitutes.

Rough tree rail Timbers along the sides forming part of the upper bulwarks.

A round turn double bitted The bitts were timber projections on the foredeck round which the anchor cable was secured, a round turn being part of the knots used. Sometimes there were two bitts—hence double bitted. Hurricane means he has been tightly secured in matrimony.

Hamilton Moore Author of a standard work on navigation published in 1776 and a naval officer's "bible", hence a sacreligious reference to the prayer book marriage ceremony.

Missed stays The nautical expression for a ship failing to go about being used to convey the absence of the female period and consequent pregnancy.

Luff Slang expression for lieutenant. An easier connection to see in the English pronunciation "lef-tenant" than in the American "loo-tenant".

Heave and paul There were pauls (modern spelling "pawls") on the capstan to prevent the anchor cable slipping back when being heaved in.

Brace up and haul aft Trim the sails in tighter for more speed—in other words she should be gone.

Coach horses Joking expression for the crew of the captain's barge.

Last up the main hatchway To encourage smartness some captains habitually punished the last man on deck or the last up the mast, etc.

CHAPTER TEN

Sidesmen Party of men drawn up to pipe the visiting captain down the side as he departs.

Abaft Word used wrongly here for "aft" or "at the stern". Strictly speaking "abaft" is positional and can only be used in relation to another object (e.g. "abaft the mainmast", etc.).

CHAPTER ELEVEN

The story of Mr. Keith's captivity among the American Indians— The events which occupy this diversionary chapter bear a strong resemblance to parts of the Pocahontas story which Davis turned into the novel "The First Settlers in Virginia".

Baron Trenk Mid 18th century European adventurer.

Fusel Light musket.

Jerry Abbreviation of Jeremiah, the pessimistic Old Testament prophet.

CHAPTER TWELVE

Hammocks in the quarterdeck nettings Readers will note how closely details of this action compare with the author's experiences in the *Artois.*

Captain of the afterguard Use of the word captain in this and similar contexts signifies a seaman responsible for a small party of men on particular duties. The Royal Navy sometimes uses the word half-jokingly (e.g. the Captain of the Heads is the bloke who cleans the lavatories).

My grog is stopped I am dying and therefore my daily allowance of rum will cease.

Well Space in the bottom of the ship into which any water ran to be removed, if possible, by the pumps.

CHAPTER THIRTEEN

Cruize The word we should use now is patrol. Cruise has come to be associated only with pleasure trips and the 'z' spelling is obsolete.

Our fortune is made Prize money remained as an incentive for the Royal Navy right down to modern times. Captured ships, naval or merchant, were sold with their cargoes and the proceeds divided into eighths. The captain received $^3/_8$th, the officers shared $^1/_8$th, and the rest of the crew (several hundreds) shared $^2/_8$ths. The flag officer responsible for the ship, even if hundreds of miles away, received $^1/_8$th. There was an instance when every seaman of one ship made the equivalent of 16 years' pay in one afternoon. A lieutenant making £500 for one prize was not uncommon and some vast sums were paid out at times.

Lead In shallow water the lead was cast to find the depth while under way. In deep water the ship was hove-to and a long deep sea lead line lowered by men stationed the length of the ship. Before modern instruments taking soundings was an important aid to navigation.

Fathom Equals six feet.

Start Point Headland in Devon. Often first landfall for vessels coming up the English Channel.

Spanker boom Spar carrying the jigger or spanker fore and aft sail. Not setting well here because the wind is dead aft.

Norfolk Packet Mail boat from Norfolk, Virginia.

CHAPTER FOURTEEN

Beachy Head Prominent chalk headland on the Sussex coast.

His agent Prize money was a complicated legal matter. Each claim had to be heard in the High Court of Admiralty and there could be rival claimants if more than one ship was at the scene of action, so naval officers employed agents ashore to look after their interests. Nelson and St. Vincent were in dispute for years through their agents.

Volunteer company Many part time militia companies were raised during the Napoleonic Wars. They often sported splendid uniforms and their exercises on the open spaces around London and elsewhere were a fashionable spectacle.

Sophonisba Name from Greek mythology.

Exchange to Hyde Park A distance of two or three miles.

Callipash and callipee Edible portions of a turtle from the upper and lower shells respectively.

CHAPTER FIFTEEN

Fore top bowline Rope leading from the fore topsail to the deck to control the leach or after edge of the sail.

Lobster lovers Derogatory reference to soldiers, from their red coats.

Make stern-way To go backwards or lose ground.

Lord Chesterfield Author of a famous book of advice for young men.

Stiver Small coin of little value.

Backing and filling Phrase used of manouevring a ship in confined waters by alternately backing sails to pay the head off, then letting them fill to move forward.

Rough-knot Simple sailor.

Hove to under storm-stay-sail Riding out a gale with only a small sail hoisted. Used here of social distress.

Bergamyhot A scented herb.

Hanger Naval slang for sword.

CHAPTER SIXTEEN

As good as a Spanish war Wars with Spain offered exceptionally good opportunities of prize money due to the large number of merchantmen carrying home silver from the Spanish possessions in South America.

Marine adrift upon a grating Gratings were slatted covers to the hatchways to admit light and air below decks.

Painter . . . on fire Derisive reference to the slovenly way the painter (line from the bow for securing the boat) was trailing in the water.

Way-enough An order to stop rowing.

Wherry The Thames was still used habitually for transport about London at this time. The usual passenger boats, known as wherries, were up to 25 feet in length with one or more attendant oarsmen.

Washboards Slang for lapels whereon insignia of rank could be seen.

Gretna Green Village just over the Scottish border which became notorious for run-away weddings. Scots marriage laws then required few formalities and the Gretna Green blacksmith was supposed to perform the ceremony.

Chops Nautical term for the entrance to a channel or estuary.

League Approximately three nautical miles.

Britannia A veteran first-rate built in 1762 and in action at St. Vincent and Trafalgar.

Head rails Curved timbers continuing the line of the bows out to the figurehead.

CHAPTER SEVENTEEN

Jemmy Linkhorn Feedle Song from a popular opera "Inkle and Yarico" by Colman 1787.

Jerusalem or the Anti-Gallican Names of two low taverns in London.

CHAPTER EIGHTEEN

Ward of Chancery A minor under the protection of the Courts.

Bends Another name for the wales or thick, shaped re-inforcing planks along the ship's side.

East of Temple Bar In the poorer district of London.

By the hookey Probably "by the anchor", a mock oath.

Epaulet Gold decoration on the shoulder of a uniform, introduced into the Royal Navy for Post Captains in 1795.

Shillela A blackthorn stick. Irish origin, properly spelled shillelagh.

Athwart our hawse For one ship to come athwart the hawse of another is for it to run foul of the bows and cable of an anchored vessel.

CHAPTER TWENTY

Henley Town on the River Thames about 25 miles upstream from London.

Calash A lady's hood, stiffened to project beyond the face.

Straits of Baffleman They appear to be fictitious.

Edinburgh Review A quarterly magazine for which John Davis had a particular hatred, because of unkind criticisms of his work.

Ycleped Old English word for "called" or "styled".

Mr. Perry An apothecary tried at Bristol in 1794 for abducting a wealthy heiress of 16. Erskine, the defending counsel, secured his acquittal after calling the Gretna blacksmith to give evidence that the girl acted of her own free will.

CHAPTER TWENTY-ONE

Pinnace Another type of ship's boat, with 8 or 16 oars and able to set a small sail.

Houri Nymph in Moslem mythology.

Playing at long bowls Engaging the enemy at long range.

My jack, my ensign, my pendant A jack is the national flag worn at the stem. The ensign at the stern was at that time the squadronal colours of the navy and the pendant at the masthead a symbol of the ship's commission.

First chop mandarines High ranking Chinese officials.

By the deep nine One of the calls made by a leadsman in reporting the depth, in this case nine fathoms. The words form the refrain of a popular sea-song.

CHAPTER TWENTY-THREE

Rodney's action with De Grasse The battle of The Saints, 1782.

James Howels An actual Caerphilly character it would seem, but nothing is now known of him.

Dreadnought Name of a ship. Dreadnought has been in use as a ship's name in the British Navy since the 16th century. It later became a generic term for iron battleships.

Fight the old soldier To shirk duty or sham sickness.

Tom Coxe's traverse A dodging way of appearing to work while doing nothing. A traverse describes the zig zag track of a ship tacking to windward, but who Tom Coxe was is now unknown.

Quill driver Office worker, or as we should say now, pen pusher.

Meat well towed Probably means made tender. The verb to tow is used of reducing rope or flax to fibres.

Cobbed Punished by striking on the backside.

Sheathing Protective material, latterly copper, over a ship's wooden bottom to prevent rot.

Dr. Goldsmith The poet Oliver Goldsmith.

CHAPTER TWENTY-FOUR

Pont y Prid, that is, New Bridge Although Pontypridd appeared on some maps as New Bridge this is not a translation of the Welsh, which would be "Beautiful Bridge".

Merthyr, etc. An interesting description of the embryonic industrial revolution in the Welsh valleys and confirmation that Davis must have travelled in South Wales between 1802 and 1804.

Pyle House This inn was highly praised by early 19th century guide books.

Chay Short for chaise, a light open carriage.

Splice the main brace Strictly, an order occasionally given in the Royal Navy, before the daily tot was abolished in 1970, to issue a double ration. Originates in the fact that the main brace was a heavy rope exceptionally difficult to splice, thus meriting a special reward. The phrase has come to mean now "let's celebrate".

Grog Grog is rum diluted with water. Officers as well as ratings received the daily ration until 1881.

Acknowledgements and Sources

The text used for this edition of "The Post Captain" follows that of the third edition of 1808. The only alteration has been to run together some of the original 46 very short chapters to make a more convenient number. Original spellings have been kept.

Information about the early publishing history of the novel comes from the introduction to the 1928 edition. Most of the facts about the author's time at sea and subsequent career are to be found scattered about his other written works in the British Library. For naval background the introductory chapters rely in the main on Michael Lewis's "Navy of Britain" and "Social History of the Royal Navy", Laird Clowes' "The Royal Navy. A History from the Earliest Times" and John Masefield's "Sea Life in Nelson's Time". In compiling the glossary recourse has been had among other works to the Oxford English Dictionary, the Oxford Companion to the Sea and Ships, the Country Life Book of Nautical Terms Under Sail and Falconer's Dictionary of the Marine.

The editor also gratefully acknowledges help kindly given by the staffs of Wiltshire County Records Office, the Berkshire County Reference Library at Reading, Wiltshire County Library's Local History Section, the National Maritime Museum, Greenwich and the Registrar of the Charterhouse.